"Look, Ava, I Know We Were Never The Best Of Friends..."

Even if we were—for one night, anyway—lovers, Peyton couldn't help thinking. Hoping she wasn't thinking that, too. Figuring she probably was. "But I obviously need help with this new and improved me, and I'm not going to get it from some total stranger. I don't know anyone here who could help me except you. Because you're the only one here who knows me."

"I *did* know you," she corrected him. "When we were in high school. Neither of us is the person we were then."

There was something in her voice when she said that that made Peyton hesitate. It was true he wasn't the person he'd been in high school; Ava obviously still was. Maybe the adult wasn't quite as snotty, vain or superficial, but she could still put a guy in his place. She was still classy.

She was still beautiful.

She was still out of his league.

My Fair Billionaire

ELIZABETH BEVARLY

First published in Great Britain 2014
by Mills & Boon, an imprint of Harlequin (UK) Limited,
Large Print edition 2014
Eton House, 18-24 Paradise Road,
Richmond, Surrey, TW9 1SR

ISBN: 978 0 263 24431 1

Harlequin (UK) Limited's policy is to use papers that are natural, renewable and recyclable products and made from wood grown in sustainable forests. The logging and manufacturing processes conform to the legal environmental regulations of the country of origin.

Printed and bound in Great Britain
by CPI Antony Rowe, Chippenham, Wiltshire

ELIZABETH BEVARLY

is a *New York Times* bestselling, RITA® Award nominated author of more than seventy novels and novellas who recently celebrated the twenty-fifth anniversary of signing her first book contract—with Mills & Boon®! Her novels have been translated into more than two dozen languages and published in more than three dozen countries, and someday she hopes to visit all the places her books have. Until then, she writes full-time in her native Louisville, Kentucky, usually on a futon between two cats. She loves reading and movies and discovering British TV shows on Netflix. And also fiddling around with soup recipes. And going to farmers' markets with her husband. And texting with her son, who's at college in Washington, D.C. Visit her website at www.elizabethbevarly.com or find her on Facebook at the Elizabeth Bevarly Reader Page.

For David and Eli.
Thanks for always having my back.
I love you guys. OXY.

One

T. S. Eliot was right, Ava Brenner thought as she quickened her stride down Michigan Avenue and ducked beneath the awning of a storefront. April really was the cruelest month. Yesterday, the skies above Chicago had been blue and clear, and temperatures hovered in the high fifties. Today, gray clouds pelted the city with freezing rain. She tugged her scarf from the collar of her trench coat and over her head, knotting it beneath her chin. The weather would probably ruin the emerald silk, but she was on her way to meet a prospective vendor and would rather replace an injured scarf than have the perfect auburn chignon at her nape get wet and ragged.

Image was everything. Bottom line. That was a lesson life hammered home when Ava was still in high school. April wasn't the only thing that was cruel—teenage girls could be downright brutal. Especially the rich, vain, snotty ones at posh private schools who wore the latest designer fashions and belittled the need-based-scholarship students who made do with discount-store markdowns.

Ava pushed the thought away. A decade and a half lay between her and graduation. She was the owner of her own business now, a boutique called Talk of the Town that rented haute couture fashions to women who wanted only the best for those special occasions in life. Even if the shop was operating on a shoestring and wishful thinking, it was starting to show a profit. At least she looked the part of successful businesswoman. No one had to know she was her own best customer.

She whipped the scarf from her head and tucked it into the pocket of her trench coat as she entered an elegant eatery. Beneath, she wore a charcoal-gray Armani jacket and trousers, paired with a sage-colored shell she knew enhanced her green eyes. The outfit had arrived at Talk of the Town just this week, and she'd wanted to test-drive it for comfort and wearability.

As she approached the host stand, her cell phone twittered. It was the vendor she was supposed to be meeting, asking to postpone their appointment for an evening later in the week. So Ava would be on her own for dinner tonight. As usual. Still, she hadn't taken herself out in a long time, and she had been working extra hard this month. She'd earned a bit of a treat.

Basilio, the restaurant's owner, greeted her by name with a warm smile. Every time she saw him, Ava was reminded of her father. Basilio had the same dark eyes, close-cropped salt-and-pepper hair and neatly trimmed mustache. But she was reasonably certain that, unlike her father, Basilio had never done time in a federal prison.

Without even checking the seating chart, he led Ava to her favorite table by the window, where she could watch the passersby as she ate.

As she lifted her menu, however, her attention was yanked away by a ruckus in the bar. When she glanced up, she saw Dennis, her favorite bartender, being berated by a customer, a tall man with broad shoulders and coal-black hair. He was evidently offended by Dennis's suggestion that he'd had too much to drink, a condition that was frankly obvious.

"I'm fine," the man insisted. Although his words weren't slurred, his voice was much louder than necessary. "And I want another Macallan. Neat."

Dennis remained calm as he replied, "I don't think—"

"That's right," the man interrupted him. "You don't think. You serve drinks. Now serve me another Macallan. Neat."

"But, Mr.—"

"Now," the man barked.

Ava's pulse leaped at the angrily uttered word. She'd worked her way through college at three jobs, one of which had been as a waitress. She'd dealt with her share of patrons who became bullies after drinking too much. Thankfully, Basilio and her waiter, Marcus, were on the spot quickly to attend to the situation.

Dennis shook his head at the others' approach, holding up a hand for them to wait. In gentling tones, he said, "Mr. Moss, maybe it would be better if you had a cup of coffee instead."

Heat splashed into Ava's belly at hearing the name. Moss. She had gone to school—long ago, in a galaxy far away—with a Moss. Peyton Moss. He had been a grade ahead of her at the tony Emerson Academy.

But this couldn't be him, she told herself. Peyton Moss had sworn to everyone at Emerson that he was leaving Chicago the moment he graduated and never coming back. And he'd kept that promise. Ava had returned to Chicago only a few months after earning her business degree and had run into a handful of her former classmates—more was the pity—none of whom had mentioned Peyton's return.

She looked at the man again. Peyton had been Emerson's star hockey player, due not just to his prowess, but also his size. His hair had been shoulder-length, inky silk, and his voice, even then, had been dark and rich. By now, it could have easily deepened to the velvety baritone of the man at the bar.

When he turned to look at Marcus, Ava bit back a gasp. Although the hair was shorter and the profile harsher, it was indeed Peyton. She'd know that face anywhere. Even after sixteen years.

Without thinking, she jumped up and hurried to place herself between Peyton and the others. With all the calm she could muster, she said, "Gentlemen. Maybe what we need here is an unbiased intermediary to sort everything out."

Peyton would laugh himself silly about that if he recognized her. Ava had been anything but *unbiased* toward him in high school. But he'd been plenty biased toward her, too. That was what happened when two people moved in such disparate social circles in an environment where the lines of society were stark, immutable and absolute. When upper class met lower class in a place like Emerson, the sparks that flew could immolate an entire socioeconomic stratum.

"Ms. Brenner, I don't think that's a good idea,"

Basilio said. “Men in his condition can be unpredictable, and he’s three times your size.”

“My condition is fine,” Peyton snapped. “Or it would be. If this establishment honored the requests of its paying customers.”

“Just let me speak to him,” Ava said, dropping her voice.

Basilio shook his head. “Marcus and I can handle this.”

“But I know him. He and I went to school together. He’ll listen to me. We’re…we were…” Somehow she pushed the word out of her mouth. “Friends.”

It was another word that would have made Peyton laugh. The two of them had been many things at Emerson—unwilling study partners, aggressive sparring partners and for one strange, intoxicating night, exuberant lovers—but never, ever, friends.

“I’m sorry, Ms. Brenner,” Basilio said, “but I can’t let you—”

Before he could stop her, Ava spun around and made her way to the bar. “Peyton,” she said when she came to a halt in front of him.

Instead of looking at Ava, he continued to study Dennis. "What?"

"This has gone far enough. You need to be reasonable."

He opened his mouth, but halted when his gaze connected with hers. She'd forgotten what beautiful eyes he had. They were the color and clarity of good cognac, fringed by sooty lashes.

"I know you," he said, suddenly more lucid. His tone was confident, but his expression held doubt. "Don't I?"

"You and I went to school together," she said, deliberately vague. "A long time ago."

He seemed surprised by the connection. "I don't remember you from Stanford."

Stanford? she echoed to herself. Last she'd heard he was headed to a university in New England with a double major in hat tricks and cross-checking and a minor in something vaguely scholastic in case he injured himself. How had he ended up on the West Coast?

"Not Stanford," she said.

"Then where?"

Reluctantly, she told him, “The Emerson Academy here in Chicago.”

His surprise multiplied. “You went to Emerson?”

Well, he didn’t need to sound so shocked. Did she still look that much like a street urchin?

“Yes,” she said evenly. “I went to Emerson.”

He narrowed his eyes as he studied her more closely. “I don’t remember you from there, either.”

Something sharp pricked her chest at the comment. She should be happy he didn’t remember her. She wished she could forget the girl she’d been at Emerson. She wished she could forget Peyton, as well. But so often over the past sixteen years, he and the other members of his social circle had crept into her brain, conjuring memories and feelings she wished she could bury forever.

Without warning, he lifted a hand to cradle her chin and jaw. Something hot and electric shot through her at the contact, but he didn’t seem to notice. He simply turned her face gently one way, then the other, looking at her from all angles. Finally, he dropped his hand back to the bar. He shook his head, opened his mouth to speak, then—

Then his expression went slack. "Oh, my God. Ava Brenner."

She expelled an irritated sigh. Damn. She didn't want anyone to remember her the way she'd been at Emerson, especially the kids like Peyton. Especially Peyton, period. In spite of that, a curl of pleasure wound through her when she realized he'd made a space for her, however small, in his memory.

Resigned, she replied, "Yes. It's me."

"Well, I'll be damned," he said, his tone belying nothing of what he might be thinking.

He collapsed onto a barstool, gazing at her with those piercing golden eyes. A rush of conflicting emotions washed over her that she hadn't felt for a very long time—pride and shame, arrogance and insecurity, blame and guilt. And in the middle of it all, an absolute uncertainty about Peyton, about herself, about the two of them together. Then as well as now.

Oh, yes. She definitely felt as if she was back

in high school. And she didn't like it now any better than she had then.

When it became clear that Peyton wasn't going to cause any more trouble, Dennis snatched the empty cocktail glass from the bar and replaced it with a coffee mug. Basilio released a slow breath and threw Ava a grateful smile. Marcus went back to check on his diners. Ava told herself to return to her table, that she'd done her good deed for the day and should just leave well enough alone. But Peyton was still staring at her, and something in his expression made her pause. Something that sent another tumble of memories somersaulting through her brain. Different memories from the others that had plagued her tonight, but memories that were every bit as unpleasant and unwanted.

Because it had been Ava, not Peyton, who had led the ruling social class at the posh, private Emerson Academy. It had been Ava, not Peyton, who had been rich, vain and snotty. It had been Ava, not Peyton, who had worn the latest designer fashions and belittled the need-based-scholarship students who made do with discount-store markdowns. At least until the summer before her senior year, when her family had lost everything, and she'd suddenly found herself walking in their discount-store markdowns herself. Then she'd been the one who was penniless, unwanted and bullied.

Peyton didn't say a word as Ava studied him, pondering all the things that had changed in the decade and a half since she'd seen him. A few threads of silver had woven their way into his dark hair, and the lower half of his face was shadowed by a day's growth of beard. She couldn't remember him shaving in high school. But perhaps he had, even if that morning when she'd woken up beside him in her bedroom, he—

She tried to stop the memories before they could form, but they came anyway. How it had all played out when the two of them were forced to work together on a semester-long project for World Civ, one of the classes that combined seniors and juniors. Money really did change everything—at least at Emerson, it had. School rules had dictated that those whose families had lots of money must belittle those whose families had none, and that those who had nothing must resent those who had everything. In spite of that, there had always been…something… between Ava and Peyton. Something hot and heavy that burned up the air in any room the two of them shared. Some strange, combustible reaction due to…something. Something weird. Something volatile. Something neither of them had ever been able to identify or understand.

Or, ultimately, resist.

It had culminated one night at her house when the two of them had been working late on that class project and had ended up… Well, it hadn't exactly been making love, since whatever they'd felt for each other then had had nothing to do with love. But it hadn't been sex, either. There had been more to it than the mingling of two bodies. It had just fallen short of the mingling of two souls.

The morning after, Peyton had jumped out of bed on one side, and Ava had leaped out on the other. They had hurled both accusations and excuses, neither listening to the other. The only thing they'd agreed on was that they'd made a colossal mistake that was never to be mentioned again. Peyton had dressed and fled through her bedroom window, not wanting to be discovered, and Ava had locked it tight behind him. Monday morning, they turned in their assignment and went back to being enemies, and Ava had held her breath for the remainder of the year. Only after Peyton graduated and took off for college had she been able to breathe again.

For all of three weeks. Until her entire life came crashing down around her, pitching her to the bottom rung of the social ladder among the very people she had treated so callously before. People whom she quickly learned had deserved none of the treatment she had spent years dishing out.

She turned to Basilio. "I need a favor. Could I ask one of your waiters to run back to my shop for my car so I can drive Mr. Moss home? I'll stay here and have coffee with him until then."

Basilio looked at her as if she'd lost every marble she possessed.

"It's only a fifteen-minute walk," she told him. "Ten if whoever you send hurries."

"But, Ms. Brenner, he's not—"

"—himself," Ava quickly interjected. "Yes, I know, which is why he deserves a pass tonight."

"Are you sure that's a good idea?"

No, she wasn't. This Peyton was a stranger to her in so many ways. Not that the Peyton she used to know had exactly been an open book. He might not have thought much of her kind when they were in high school, and maybe he hadn't been much of a gentleman, but he hadn't been dangerous, either. Well, not in the usual sense of the word. Whatever had made him behave badly tonight, he'd calmed down once he recognized a familiar face.

Besides, she owed him. She owed him more than she could ever make up for. But at least, by doing this, she might make some small start.

"My keys are in my purse at my table," she told Basilio, "and my car is parked behind the shop. Just send someone down there to get it, and I'll take him home. Please," she added.

Basilio looked as if he wanted to object again, but instead said, "Fine. I'll send Marcus. I just hope you know what you're doing."

Yes, well, that, Ava thought, made two of them.

* * *

Peyton Moss awoke the way he hadn't awoken in a very long time—hungover. Really hungover. When he opened his eyes, he had no idea where he was or what time it was or what he'd been doing in the hours before wherever and whatever time he was in.

He lay still in bed for a minute—he was at least in a bed, wasn't he?—and tried to figure out how he'd arrived in his current position. Hmm. Evidently, his current position was on his stomach atop a crush of sheets, his face shoved into a pillow. So that would be a big yep on the bed thing. The question now was, *whose* bed? Especially since, whoever the owner was, she wasn't currently in it with him.

But he concluded the owner of the bed must be a she. Not only did the sheets smell way too good to belong to a man, but the wallpaper, he discovered when he rolled over, was covered with roses, and a chandelier above him dripped ropes of crystal beads. He drove his gaze around the room and saw more evidence of gender bias in an ultrafeminine dresser and armoire, shoved into a corner by the room's only window, which was covered by billows of lace.

So he'd gone home with a strange woman last night. Nothing new about that, except that going home with strangers was something he'd been more likely to do in his youth. Not that thirty-four was old, dammit, but it was an age when a man was expected to start settling down and figuring out what he wanted. Not that Peyton hadn't done that, too, but… Okay, so maybe he hadn't settled down that much. And maybe he hadn't quite figured out everything he wanted. He'd settled some and figured out the bulk of it. Hell, that was why he'd come back to a city he'd sworn he would never set foot in again.

Chicago. God. The last time he was here, he'd been eighteen years old and wild as a rabid badger. He'd left his graduation ceremony and gone straight to the bus station, stopping only long enough to cram his cap and gown into the first garbage can he could find. He hadn't even gone home to say goodbye. Hell, no one at home had given a damn what he did. No one in Chicago had.

He draped an arm over his eyes and expelled a weary sigh. Yeah, nothing like a little adolescent melodrama to start the day off right.

He jackknifed to a sitting position and slung his legs over the bed. His jacket and tie were hanging over the back of a chair and his shoes were on the floor near his feet. His rumpled shirt and trousers were all fastened, as was his belt. Obviously, nothing untoward had happened the night before, so, with any luck, there wouldn't be any awkward moments once he found out who his hostess was.

Carefully, he made his way to the door and headed into a bathroom on his right, turning on the water to fill the sink. After splashing a few handfuls onto his face, he felt a little better. He still looked like hell, he noted when he caught his reflection in the mirror. But he felt a little better.

The mirror opened to reveal a slim cabinet behind it, and he was grateful to see a bottle of mouthwash. At least that took care of the dead-animal taste in his mouth. He found a comb, too, and dragged that through his hair, then did his best to smooth the wrinkles from his shirt.

Leaving the bathroom, he detected the aroma of coffee and followed it to a kitchen that was roughly the size of an electron. The light above the stove was on, allowing him to find his way around. The only wall decoration was a calendar with scenes of Italy, but the fridge door was crowded with stuff—a notice about an upcoming Italian film festival at the Patio Theater, some pictures of women's clothing cut out of a magazine and a postcard reminding whoever lived here of an appointment with her gynecologist.

The coffeemaker must have been on a timer, because there was no evidence of anyone stirring but him. Glancing down at his watch, he saw that it was just after five, which helped explain why no one was stirring. Except that the coffeemaker timer must have been set for now, so whoever lived here was normally up at this ungodly hour.

He crossed the kitchen in a single stride and exited on the other side, finding himself in a living room that was barely as big as the bedroom.

Enough light from the street filtered through the closed curtains for him to make out a lamp on the other side of the room, and he was about to move toward it when a sound to his right stopped him. It was the sound a woman made upon stirring when she was not ready to stir, a soft sough of breath tempered by a fretful whimper. Through the semidarkness, he could just make out the figure of a woman lying on the couch.

Peyton had found himself in a lot of untenable positions over the years—many of which had included women—but he had no idea what to do in a situation like this. He didn't know where he was, had no idea how he'd gotten here and was clueless about the identity of the woman under whose roof he had passed the night. For all he knew, she could be married. Hell, for all he knew, she could be a knife-wielding maniac. Then his hostess made that quiet sound of semi-consciousness again, and he decided she couldn't be the last. Knife-wielding maniacs couldn't sound that delectable. Still, if she was sleeping out here and he'd spent the night in her bedroom, he had nothing to feel guilty about, right? Except for tossing her out of her bed when he should have been the one sleeping on the couch. And except for passing out on her in the first place.

What the hell had happened last night? He mentally retraced his steps from the moment he set foot back on his native soil. Although he'd left Chicago via Greyhound bus more than fifteen years ago, his return had been aboard a private jet. His private jet. He might have been a street dog in his youth, but in adulthood… Ah, who was he kidding? In adulthood, he was still a street dog. That was the reason he was back here.

Anyway, after landing, he'd headed straight to the Hotel Intercontinental on Michigan Avenue. That much Peyton remembered with crystal clarity, because the Hotel Intercontinental was the sort of place that A) he never would have had the nerve to enter when he was a kid, and B) would have tossed him out on his ass if he *had* tried to enter when he was a kid. Funny how they'd had no problem accepting his platinum card yesterday.

He further remembered walking into his suite and tossing his bag onto the massive bed, then going to the window and pushing aside the curtains. He recalled looking out on Michigan Avenue, at the gleaming high-rises and upscale department stores that had always seemed off-limits to him when he lived here. This whole neighborhood had seemed off-limits to him when he was a kid. In spite of that, he'd come to this part of town five days a week, nine months a year, because the Emerson Academy for College Preparatory Learning sat in the middle of it. For those other two days of the week and three months of the year, though, Peyton had always had to stay with his own kind in the rough South Side neighborhood where he'd grown up.

Yesterday, looking out that window, he had been brutally reminded of how his teenage life in this part of town had been juxtaposed to the life—if he could even call it that—that he'd led in his not-even-marginal neighborhood. As much as he'd hated Emerson, it had always felt good to escape his home life for eight hours a day. Yesterday, looking out at the conspicuous consumption of Michigan Avenue, Peyton had, ironically, been transported back to his old neighborhood instead. He'd been able to smell the grease and gasoline of the garage he and his old man had lived above—and where he'd worked to save money for college when he wasn't at school. He'd heard the police sirens that pelted the crumbling urban landscape, had seen the roving packs of gangs that considered his block fair game. He'd felt the grime on his skin and tasted the soot that belched from the factory smokestacks. And then…

Then had come memories of Emerson, where he'd won a spot on the school hockey team—along with a full scholarship—thanks to his above-average grades and his ruthlessness on the rink. God, he'd hated that school, teeming as it had been with blue-blooded trust-fund babies who were way too rich for his system. But he'd loved how clean and bright the place was, and how it smelled like floor wax and Calvin Klein perfume. He'd liked the quiet during classes and how orderly everything ran. He'd liked being able to eat one decent meal a day. He'd liked feeling safe, if only for a little while.

Not that he would have admitted any of that

back then. Not that he would admit it to anyone now. But he'd been smart enough to know that an education from a place like Emerson would look a hell of a lot better on a college application than the decaying public school he would have attended otherwise. He'd stomached the rich kids—barely—by finding the handful of other students like himself. The wretched refuse. The other scholarship kids who were smart but poor and determined to end up in a better place than their parents. There had been maybe ten of them in a school where they were outnumbered a hundred to one. Peyton hadn't given a damn about those hundreds. Except for one, who had gotten under his skin and stayed there.

Ava Brenner. The Golden Girl of the Gold Coast. Her daddy was so rich and so powerful, and she was so snotty and so beautiful, she'd ruled that school. Not a day had passed at Emerson that didn't revolve around Ava and her circle of friends—all handpicked by the princess herself, and all on eggshells knowing they could be exiled at her slightest whim. Not a day had passed that Peyton hadn't had to watch her strolling down the hall, flipping that sweep of red-gold hair around as if it was spun copper… and looking at him as if he were something disgusting stuck to the bottom of her shoe. And not a day had passed when he hadn't wanted her. Badly. Even knowing she was spoiled and shallow and vain.

He opened his eyes. Yeah, he remembered now that he had been thinking about Ava yesterday. In fact, that was what had made him beat a hasty retreat to the hotel bar. He remembered that, too. And he remembered tossing back three single malts on an empty stomach in rapid succession. He remembered being politely asked to leave the hotel bar and, surprisingly, complying. He remembered lurching out onto Michigan Avenue and looking for the first place he could find to get another drink, then being steady enough on his feet to convince the bartender to fix him a couple more. Then…

He tried harder to remember what had happened after that. But all he could recall was a husky—sexy—voice, and the soft scent of gardenias, and a pair of beautiful sea-green eyes, all of which had seemed oddly familiar somehow.

That brought his gaze back to the woman sleeping on the couch. In the semidarkness, he could see that she lay on her side, facing the room, one hand curled in front of her face. The blanket with which she had covered herself was drooping, part of it pooled on the floor. For some reason, he was compelled to move to the couch and pick it up, to drape it across her sleeping form. As he bent over her, he inhaled the faint scent of gardenias again, as if it had followed him out of his memories.

And just like that, he was pummeled by another one.

Ava Brenner. Again. She was the one who had smelled of gardenias. Peyton remembered the night the two of them had— Well, the night they'd had to finish a school project together at her house. In her room. When her parents were out of town. At one point, she'd gone downstairs to fix them something to eat, and he'd taken advantage of her absence to shamelessly prowl around her room, opening her closet and dresser drawers, snooping for anything he could discover about her. When he came across her underwear drawer, he actually stole a pair of her panties. Pale yellow silk. God help him, he still had them. As he'd stuffed them into his back pocket that night, his gaze lit on a bottle of perfume on her dresser. Night Gardenia, it was called. That was the only way he knew that what she smelled like was gardenias. He'd never smelled—or even seen—one before that night.

As he draped the cover over the sleeping woman, his gaze fell to her face, and his gut clenched tight. He told himself he was imagining things. He was just so overcome with memories of Ava that he was imprinting her face onto that of a stranger. The odds of him running into the last person he wanted to see in Chicago—within hours of his arrival—were too ridiculous to compute. There were two and a half million people in this city. No way could fate be that cruel. No way would he be thrown back into the path of—

Before the thought even formed in his head, though, Peyton knew. It was her. Ava Brenner. Golden Girl of the Gold Coast. Absolute ruler of the Emerson Academy for College Preparatory Learning. A recurring character in the most feverish dreams he'd ever had as a teenage boy.

And someone he'd hoped he would never, ever see again.

Two

"Ava?"

As if he'd uttered an incantation to free a fairy-tale princess from an evil spell, her eyes fluttered open. He tried one last time to convince himself he was only imagining her. But even in the semidarkness, he could see that it was Ava. And that she was more beautiful than he remembered.

"Peyton?" she said as she pushed herself up from the sofa.

He stumbled backward and into a chair on the other side of the room. Oh, God. Her voice. The way she said his name. It was the same way she'd said it that morning in her bedroom, when he'd opened his eyes to realize the frenetic dream he'd had about the two of them having sex hadn't been a dream at all. The panic that welled up in him now was identical to the feeling he had then, an explosion of fear and uncertainty and insecurity. He *hated* that feeling. He hadn't felt it since…

Ah, hell. He hadn't felt it since that morning in Ava's bedroom.

Don't panic, he told himself. He wasn't an eighteen-year-old kid whose only value lay in his ruthlessness on the rink. He wasn't living in poverty with a drunk for a father after his mother had deserted them both. He sure as hell wasn't the refuse of the Emerson Academy who wasn't worthy of Ava Brenner.

"Um, hi? I guess?" she said as she sat up, pulling up her covers as if she were cloaking herself in some kind of protective device. She was obviously just as anxious about seeing him as he was about seeing her.

As much as Peyton told himself to reply with a

breezy, unconcerned greeting, all he could manage was another quiet "Ava."

She pulled one hand out of her cocoon to switch on a lamp by the sofa. He squinted at the sudden brightness but didn't glance away. Her eyes seemed larger than he remembered, and the hard angles of her cheekbones had mellowed to slender curves. Her hair was shorter, darker than in high school, but still danced around her shoulders unfettered. And her mouth—that mouth that had inspired teenage boys to commit mayhem—was… Hell. It still inspired mayhem. Only now that Peyton was a man, *mayhem* took on a whole new meaning.

"You want coffee?" she asked. "It should be ready. I set the coffeemaker for the usual time, thinking I would wake up when I normally do, but I don't think it's been sitting too long. If memory serves, you like it strong, anyway."

If memory serves, he echoed to himself. She had brewed a pot of coffee for them at her house that night, in preparation for the all-nighter they knew lay ahead. He had told her he liked it strong. She remembered. Even though the two of them had barely spoken to each other after that night. Did that mean something? Did he want it to?

"Coffee sounds good," he said. "But I can get it. You take yours with cream and sugar, if *I* recall correctly."

Okay, okay. So Ava wasn't the only one who could remember that night in detail. That didn't mean anything.

She pulled the covers more snugly around herself. "Thanks."

Peyton hurried to the kitchen, grateful for the opportunity to collect himself. Ava Brenner. Damn. It was as if he'd turned on some kind of homing device the minute he got into town in order to locate her. Or maybe she had turned on one to locate him. Nah. No way would she be looking for him after all this time. She'd made her feelings for him crystal clear back at Emerson. They'd only shone with an even starker clarity after that night at her parents' house. And no way would he be looking for her, either. It was nothing but a vicious twist of fate or a vengeful God or bad karma that had brought them together again.

By the time he carried their coffee back to the living room, she had swept her hair atop her head into a lopsided knot that, amazingly, made her look even more beautiful. The covers had fallen enough to reveal a pair of flannel pajamas, decorated with multicolored polka dots. Never in a million years would he have envisioned Ava Brenner in flannel polka dots. Weirdly, though, they suited her.

She mumbled her thanks as he handed her her coffee—and he told himself he did *not* linger long enough to skim his fingers over hers to see if she felt as soft as he remembered, even if he did notice she felt softer than he remembered. He briefly entertained the idea of sitting down beside her on the couch but thankfully came to his senses and returned to the chair.

When he trusted himself not to screw up the question, he asked, "Wanna tell me how I ended up spending the night with you again?"

He winced inwardly. He really hadn't wanted to make any reference to that night in high school. But her head snapped up at the question. Obviously, she'd picked up on the allusion, too.

"You don't remember?" she asked.

There was an interesting ambiguity to the question. She could have been asking about last night or that night sixteen years ago. Of course she must have meant last night. Still, there was an interesting ambiguity.

He shook his head. As much as it embarrassed him to admit it, he told her, "No. I don't remember much of anything after arriving at some restaurant on Michigan Avenue."

Except, of course, for fleeting recollections of green eyes, soft touches and the faint aroma of gardenias. But she didn't have to know that.

"So you do remember what happened before that?" she asked.

"Yeah." Not that he was going to tell her any of that, either.

She waited for him to elaborate. He elaborated by lifting one eyebrow and saying nothing.

She sighed and tried again. "When did you get back in town?"

"Yesterday."

"You came in from San Francisco?"

The question surprised him. "How did you know?"

"When I offered to take you home last night, you told me I was going to have a long drive. Then you told me you live in an area called Sea Cliff in San Francisco. Sounds like a nice neighborhood."

That was an understatement. Sea Cliff was one of San Francisco's most expensive and exclusive communities, filled with lush properties and massive estates. His two closest neighbors were a globally known publishing magnate and a retired '60s rock and roll icon.

"It's not bad," he said evasively.

"So what took you to the West Coast?"

"Work." Before she could ask more, he turned the tables. "Still living in the Gold Coast?"

For some reason, she stiffened at the question. "No. My folks sold that house around the time I graduated from high school."

"Guess they figured those seven thousand square feet would be too much for two people instead of three. Not including the servants, of course."

She dropped her gaze to her coffee. "Only two of our staff lived on site."

"Well, then. I stand corrected." He looked around the tiny living room, recalled the tiny kitchen and tiny bedroom. "So what's this place?"

"It's…" She glanced up, hesitated, then looked down into her coffee again. "I own the shop downstairs. A boutique. Women's designer fashions."

He nodded. "Ah. So this apartment came with the place, huh?"

"Something like that."

"Easier to bring me here than to someplace where you might have to explain my presence, huh?"

For the first time, it occurred to him that Ava might be married. Hell, why wouldn't she be? She'd had every guy at Emerson panting after her. His gaze fell to the hands wrapped around her coffee mug. No rings. Anywhere. Another interesting tidbit. She'd always worn jewelry in high school. Diamond earrings, ruby and sapphire rings—they were her parents' birthstones, he'd once heard her tell a friend—and an emerald necklace that set off her eyes beautifully.

Before he had a chance to decide whether her ringless state meant she wasn't married or she just removed her jewelry at night, she said, "Well, you're not exactly an easy person to explain, are you, Peyton?"

He decided not to speculate on the remark and instead asked about her status point-blank. "Husband wouldn't approve?"

Down went her gaze again. "I'm not married."

"But you still have someone waiting for you at home that you'd have to explain me to, is that it?"

The fact that she didn't respond bothered Peyton a lot more than it should have. He told himself to move along, to just get the condensed version of last night's events and call a cab. He told himself there was nothing about Ava he wanted to know, nothing she could say that would affect his life now. He told himself to remember how bad things were between them in high school for years, not how good things were that one night.

He told himself all those things. But, as was so often the case, he didn't listen to a single word he said.

Ava did her best to reassure herself that she wasn't lying to Peyton. Lies of omission weren't really lies, were they? And what was she supposed to do? No way had she wanted him to see the postage stamp-size apartment she called home. She was supposed to be a massive success by now. She was supposed to have a posh address in the Gold Coast, a closet full of designer clothes and drawers full of designer jewelry. Well, okay, she did have those last two. But they belonged to the shop, not her. She could barely afford to rent them herself.

People believed what they wanted to believe, anyway. Even sitting in her crappy apartment, Peyton assumed she was the same dazzling—if vain, shallow and snotty—Gold Coast heiress who'd had everyone wrapped around her finger in high school. He thought she still lived in a place like the massive Georgian townhouse on Division Street where she grew up, and she still drove a car like the cream-colored Mercedes convertible she'd received for her sixteenth birthday.

He obviously hadn't heard how the Brenners of the Gold Coast had been reduced to a state of poverty and hardship that rivaled the one he'd escaped on the South Side. He didn't know her father was still doing time in a federal prison for tax evasion, embezzlement and a string of other charges, because he'd had to support a drug-and-call-girl habit. He didn't know her mother had passed away in a mental hospital after too many years of trying to cope with the anguish and ostracism brought on by her husband's betrayal. He didn't know how, before that, Colette Brenner had left Ava's father and taken her to Milwaukee to finish high school, or that Ava had done so in a school much like Emerson—except that *she* had been the poor scholarship student looked down on by the ruling class of rich kids, the same way she had looked down on Peyton and his crowd at Emerson.

Sometimes karma was a really mean schoolgirl.

But that was all the more reason she didn't

want Peyton to know the truth now. She'd barely made a dent in her karmic debt. Spending her senior year of high school walking in the shoes of the students she'd treated so shabbily for years—being treated so shabbily herself—she had learned a major life lesson. It was only one reason she'd opened Talk of the Town: so that women who hadn't had the same advantages in life that she'd taken for granted could have the chance to walk in the designer shoes of high society, if only for a little while.

It was something she was sure Peyton would understand—if it came from anyone but Ava. If he found out what she'd gone through her senior year of high school, he'd mock her mercilessly. Not that she didn't deserve it. But a person liked to have a little warning before she found herself in a situation like that. A person needed a little time to put on her protective armor. Especially a person who knew what a formidable force Peyton Moss could be.

"There's no one waiting for me at home," she said softly in response to his question.

Or anywhere else, for that matter. No one in

her former circle of friends had wanted anything to do with her once she started living below the poverty line, and she'd stepped on too many toes outside that circle for anyone there to ever want to speak to her. Peyton would be no exception.

When she looked up again, he was studying her with a scrutiny that made her uncomfortable. But all he said was, "So what did happen last night?"

"You were in Basilio's when I got there. I heard shouting in the bar and saw Dennis—he's the bartender," she added parenthetically, "talking to you. He suggested, um, that you might want a cup of coffee instead of another drink."

Instead of asking about the conversation, Peyton asked, "You know the bartender by name?"

"Sure. And Basilio, the owner, and Marcus, the waiter who helped me get you to the car. I eat at that restaurant a lot." It was the only one in the neighborhood she could afford when it came to entertaining potential clients and vendors. Not that she would admit that to Peyton.

He nodded. "Of course you eat there a lot.

Why cook for yourself when you can pay someone else do it?"

Ava ignored the comment. Peyton really was going to believe whatever he wanted about her. It didn't occur to him that sixteen years could mature a person and make her less shallow and more compassionate. Sixteen years evidently hadn't matured him, if he was still so ready to think the worst of her.

"Anyway," she continued, "you took exception to Dennis's suggestion that you'd had too much to drink—and you *had* had too much to drink, Peyton—and you got a little…belligerent."

"Belligerent?" he snapped. "I never get belligerent."

Somehow Ava refrained from comment.

He seemed to realize what she was thinking, because he amended, "Anymore. It's been a long time since I was belligerent with anyone."

Yeah, probably about sixteen years. Once he graduated from Emerson, all the targets of his belligerence—especially Ava Brenner—would have been out of his life.

"Basilio was going to throw you out, but I…I

mean, when I realized you were someone I knew…I…" She expelled a restless sound. "I told him you and I are… That we were—" Somehow, she managed not to choke on the words. "Old friends. And I offered to drive you home."

"And he let you?" Peyton asked. "He let you leave with some belligerent guy he didn't know from Adam? Wow. I guess he really didn't want to offend the regular cash cow."

Bristling, Ava told him, "He let me because you calmed down a lot after you recognized me. By the time Marcus and I got you into the car, you were actually being kind of nice. I know—hard to believe."

There. Take *that,* Mr. Belligerent Cow-Caller.

"But once you were in the car," she hurried on before he could comment, "you passed out. I didn't have any choice but to bring you here. I roused you enough to get you into the apartment, but while I was setting up the coffee, you found your way to the bedroom and went out like a light again. I thought maybe you'd sleep it off in a few hours, but… Well. That didn't happen."

"I've been working a lot the last few weeks," he

said shortly, "on a demanding project. I haven't gotten much sleep."

"You were also blotto," she reminded him. Mostly because the cow comment still stung.

In spite of that, she wondered what kind of work he did and how he'd spent his life since they graduated. How long had he been in San Francisco? Was he married? Did he have children? Even as Ava told herself it didn't matter, she was helpless not to glance at his left hand. No ring. No indentation or tan line to suggest one had ever been there. Not that that was any definer of status. Even if he wasn't married, that didn't mean there wasn't a woman who was important in his life.

Not that Ava cared about any of that. She didn't. Really. All she cared about was getting him out of her hair. Getting him out of her apartment. Getting him out of her life.

In spite of that, she heard herself ask, "So why *are* you back in Chicago?"

He hesitated, as if he were trying to figure out how to reply. Finally, he said, "I'm here because my board of directors made me come."

Board of directors? she thought incredulously. *He* had a board of directors? “Board of directors?” she asked. “*You* have a board of directors?”

The question sounded even worse coming out of her mouth than it had sitting in her head, where it had sounded pretty bad.

Before she had a chance to apologize, Peyton told her—with a glare that could have boiled an ice cube, “Yeah, Ava. I have a board of directors. They’re part of the multimillion-dollar corporation of which I am chief shareholder, not to mention CEO. A company that’s named after me. On account of, in case I didn’t mention it, I own it.”

Ava grew more astonished with every word he spoke. But her surprise wasn’t from the discovery that he was an enormous success—she’d always known Peyton could do or be whatever he wanted. She just hadn’t pegged him for becoming the corporate type. On the contrary, he’d always scorned the corporate world. He’d scorned anyone who strove to make lots of money. He’d despised people like the ones in Ava’s social circle. And now he was one of them?

This time, however, she kept her astonishment to herself.

At least, she thought she did, until he added, "You don't have to look so shocked. I did have one or two redeeming qualities back in high school, not the least of which was a work ethic."

"Peyton, I didn't mean—"

"The hell you didn't." Before she could continue, he added, "In fact, Moss Holdings Incorporated is close to becoming a *billion*-dollar corporation. The only thing standing between me and those extra zeroes after my net worth is a little company in Mississippi called Montgomery and Sons. Except that it's not owned by Montgomery or his sons anymore. They all died more than a century ago. It's now owned by the Montgomery sons' granddaughters. Who are both in their eighties."

Ava had no idea what to say. Not that he seemed to expect a response from her, because he suddenly became agitated and rose from the chair to pace the room.

He sounded agitated, too, when he continued, "Helen and Dorothy Montgomery. They're sweet little old Southern ladies who wear hats and white gloves to corporate meetings and send holiday baskets to everyone every year filled with preserves and socks they make themselves. They're kind of legendary in the business and financial communities."

He stopped pacing, looking at something near the front door that Ava couldn't see. At something he probably couldn't see, either, since whatever it was must have existed far away from the apartment.

"Yeah, everybody loves the Montgomery sisters," he muttered. "They're so sweet and little and old and Southern. So I'm going to look like a bully and a jerk when I go after their company with my usual…how did the *Financial Times* put it?" He hesitated, feigning thought. "Oh, yeah. Now I remember. With my usual 'coldhearted, mind-numbing ruthlessness.' And no one will ever want to do business with me again."

Now he looked at Ava. Actually, he glared at Ava, as if all of this—whatever *this* was—was her fault. "Not that there are many in the business and financial communities who like me much now. But at least they do business with me. If they know what's good for them."

Even though she wasn't sure she was meant to be a part of this conversation, she asked, "Then why are you going after the Montgomerys' company? With ruthlessness or otherwise?"

Peyton sat down again, still looking agitated. "Because that's what Moss Holdings does. It's what *I* do. I go after failing companies and acquire them for a fraction of what they're worth, then make them profitable again. Mostly by shedding what's unnecessary, like people and benefits. Then I sell those companies to someone else for a huge profit. Or else I dismantle them and sell off their parts to the highest bidder for a pile of cash. Either way, I'm not the kind of guy people like to see coming. Because it means the end of jobs, traditions and a way of life."

In other words, she translated, what he did led to the dissolution of careers and income, plunging people into the sort of environment he'd had to claw his way out of when he was a teenager.

"Then why do you do it?" she asked.

His answer was swift and to the point. “Because it makes me huge profits and piles of cash.”

She would have asked him why making money was so important that he would destroy jobs and alienate people, but she already knew the answer. People who grew up poor and underprivileged often made making money their highest priority. Many thought if they just had enough money, it would make everything in their life all right and expurgate feelings of want and need. Some were driven enough to become tremendous successes—at making money, anyway. As far as making everything in their life right and expurgating feelings of want and need, well…that was a bit trickier.

Funnily, it was often people like Ava, who had grown up with money and been afforded every privilege, who realized how wrong such a belief was. Money didn’t make everything all right, and it didn’t expurgate feelings of anything. Sure, it could ease a lot of life’s problems. But it didn’t change who a person was at her core. It didn’t magically chase away bad feelings or alleviate stresses. It didn’t make other people respect or admire or love you. At least not for the right reasons. And it didn't bring with it the promise of…well, anything.

"And jeez, why am I even telling you all this?" Peyton said with exasperation.

Although she was pretty sure he didn't expect an answer for that, either, Ava told him, "I don't know. Maybe because you need to vent? Although why would you need to vent about a business deal, seeing as you make them all the time? Unless there's something about this particular business deal that's making you feel like… how did you put it? A bully and a jerk."

"Anyway," he said, ignoring the analysis, "for the sake of good PR and potential future projects, my board of directors thought it would be better to not go after the Montgomery sisters the way I usually go after a company—by yanking it out from under its unsuspecting owners. They think I should try to—" he made a restless gesture "—to…finesse it out from under them with my charm and geniality."

Somehow, the words *finesse* and *Peyton Moss* just didn't fit, never mind the charm and geniality stuff. Ava did manage to keep her mouth shut this time. But he seemed to need to talk about what had brought him back here, and for some reason, she hesitated to stop him.

"The BoD think it will be easier to fend off lawsuits and union problems if I can charm the company away from the Montgomerys instead of grabbing it from them. So they sent me back here to, and I quote, 'exorcise your street demons, Peyton, and learn to be a gentleman.' They've even set me up with some Henry Higgins type who's supposed to whip me into shape. Then, when I'm all nice and polished, they'll let me come back to San Francisco and go after Montgomery and Sons. But *nicely,*" he added wryly. "That way, my tarnished reputation will stay only tarnished and not firebombed into oblivion."

Now he looked at Ava as if he were actually awaiting a reply. Not that she had one to give him. Although she was finally beginning to understand what had brought him back to Chicago—kind of—she wasn't sure what he expected her to say. Certainly Peyton Moss hadn't been bred to be a gentleman. That didn't mean he wasn't capable of becoming one. Eventually. Under the right tutelage. Which even Ava was having a hard time trying to imagine.

When she said nothing, he added quietly, "But you wanna hear the real kicker?"

She did, actually—more than she probably should admit.

"The real kicker is that they think I should pick up a wife while I'm here. They've even set me up with one of those millionaire matchmakers who's supposed to introduce me to—" he took a deep breath and released it slowly, as if he were about to reveal something of great importance "—the right kind of woman."

Ava's first reaction was an odd sort of relief that he wasn't already in a committed relationship. Her second reaction was an even odder disappointment that that was about to change. There was just something about the thought of Peyton being introduced to the "right kind of woman"—meaning, presumably, the kind of woman she herself was supposed to have grown up to be—that did something funny to her insides.

He added, “They think the Montgomery sisters might look more favorably at their family business being appropriated by another family than they would having it go to a coldhearted single guy like me.” He smiled grimly. “So to finally answer your question, Ava, I’m back in Chicago to erase all evidence of my embarrassing, low-life past and learn to be a gentleman in polite society. And I’m supposed to find a nice society girl who will give me an added aura of respectability.”

Ava couldn’t quite keep the flatness from her voice when she replied, “Well, then. I hope you, in that society, with that nice society girl, will be very happy.”

“Aw, whatsamatter, Ava?” he asked in the same cool tone. “Can’t stand the fact that you and I are now social and financial equals?”

“Peyton, that’s not—”

“Yeah, there goes the neighborhood.”

“Peyton, I didn’t mean—”

"Once you start letting in the riffraff, the whole place goes to hell, doesn't it?"

Ava stopped trying to explain or apologize, since he clearly wasn't going to let her do either. What was funny—or would have been, had it not been so biting—was that they actually weren't social and financial equals. Ava was so far below him on both ladders, she wouldn't even be hit by the loose change spilling out of his pockets.

"So what about you?" he asked.

The change of subject jarred her. "What about me?"

"What are you doing now? I remember you wanted to go to Wellesley. You were going to major in art or something."

She couldn't believe he remembered her top college choice. She'd almost forgotten it herself. She hadn't allowed herself to think about things like that once the family fortune evaporated. Although Ava had been smart, she'd been a lazy student. Why worry about grades when she had parents with enough money and connections to ensure admission into any school she wanted? The only reason she'd been accepted at her tony private school in Milwaukee was that she'd tested so high on its entry exam.

How was she supposed to tell Peyton she'd ended up studying business at a community college? Not that she hadn't received a fine education, but it was a far cry from the hallowed halls of academia for which she'd originally aimed.

"English," she said evasively. "I wanted to major in English."

He nodded. "Right. So where'd you end up going?"

"Wisconsin," she said, being deliberately vague. Let him think she was talking about the university, not the state.

He arched his brows in surprise. "University of Wisconsin? Interesting choice."

"The University of Wisconsin has an excellent English department," she said. Which was true. She just hadn't been a part of it herself. Nor had she lied to Peyton, she assured herself. She never said she went to University of Wisconsin. He'd just assumed, the same way he'd made lots of other assumptions about her. Why correct him? He'd be out of her life in a matter of minutes.

"And now you own a clothing store," he said. "Good to see you putting that English degree to good use. Then again, it's not like you actually work there, is it? Now that I think about it, I guess English is a good major for an heiress. Seeing as you don't have to earn a living like the rest of us working stiffs."

Ava bit her tongue instead of defending herself. She still had a tiny spark of pride that prohibited her from telling him the truth about her situation. Okay, there was that, and also the fear that he would gloat relentlessly once he found out how she'd gone from riches to rags.

"Have you finished your coffee?" she asked. It was the most polite way she knew how to say *beat it.*

He looked down into his mug. "Yeah. I'm finished."

But he made no move to leave. Ava studied him again, considering everything she had learned. He'd achieved all his success in barely a decade's time. She'd been out of school almost as long as he, but she was still struggling to make ends meet. And she would consider herself ambitious. Yet he'd gone so much further in the same length of time. That went beyond ambitious. That was…

Well, that was Peyton.

Still, she never would have guessed his stratospheric status had he not told her. When she'd removed his jacket and shoes last night, she had noted their manufacturers—it was inescapable in her line of work. Both could have been purchased in any department store. His hair was shorter than it had been in high school, but he didn't look as if he'd paid a fortune for the cut, the way most men in his position would. He might be worth almost a billion dollars now—and don't think that realization didn't stop her heart a little—but he didn't seem to be living any differently than any other man.

But then, Peyton wasn't the kind of guy to put on airs, either.

When he stood, he hesitated, as if he wanted to say something. But he went to the kitchen without a word. She heard him rinse his cup and set it in the drainer, then move back to her bedroom. When he emerged, he was wearing his shoes and jacket, but his necktie hung loose from his collar. He looked like a man who'd had too much to drink the night before and slept in a bed other than his own. But even that couldn't detract from his appeal.

And there was the hell of it. Peyton did still appeal. He appealed to something deep inside Ava that had lain dormant for too long, something she wasn't sure would ever be able to resist him. Thankfully, that part of her wasn't the dominant part. She *could* resist Peyton Moss. Provided he left now and never came back.

For a moment, they only gazed at each other in silence. There were so many things Ava wanted to say, so many things she wanted him to know. About what had happened to her family that long-ago summer and how her senior year had changed her. About the life she led now. But she couldn't find the words. Everything came out sounding self-pitying or defensive or weak. She couldn't tolerate the idea of Peyton thinking she was any of those things.

Finally—thankfully—he ended the silence. "Thanks, Ava, for…for making sure I didn't spend last night in an alley somewhere."

"I'm sure you would have done the same for me."

He neither agreed nor disagreed. He only made his way to the front door, opened it and stepped over the threshold. She thought for a moment that he was going to leave without saying goodbye, the way he had sixteen years ago. But as he started to pull the door closed, he turned and looked at her.

"It was…interesting…seeing you again."

Yes, it had certainly been that.

"Goodbye, Peyton," she said. "I'm glad you're—"

What? she asked herself. Finally, because she knew too long a hesitation would make her look insincere, she finished, "Doing well. I'm glad you're doing well."

"Yeah, doing well," he muttered. "I'm sure as hell that."

The comment was curious. He sounded kind of sarcastic, but why would he think otherwise? He had everything he'd striven to achieve. Before she could say another word, however, the door closed with a soft click. And then, as he had been sixteen years ago, Peyton was gone.

And he hadn't said goodbye.

Three

It wasn't often that Ava heard a man's voice in Talk of the Town. So when it became clear that the rich baritone coming from beyond her office door didn't belong to anyone delivering mail or freight, her concentration was pulled from next month's employee schedule to the sales floor instead. Particularly when she recognized the man's voice as Peyton's.

No sooner did recognition dawn, however, than Lucy, one of her full-time salesclerks, poked her dark head through the office door. "There's a man out here looking for you, Ava," she said, adjusting her little black glasses. "A Mr.

Moss? He seemed surprised when I told him you were here." She lowered her voice as she added, "He was kind of fishing for your phone number. Which of course I would never give out." She smiled and lowered her voice to a stage whisper. "You might want to come out and talk to him. He's pretty yummy."

Ava sighed inwardly. Clearly, Peyton hadn't lost his ability to go from zero to sixty on the charm scale in two seconds flat.

What was he doing here? Five days had passed since their exchange in her apartment, not one of which had ended without her thinking about all the things she wished she'd said to him. She'd always promised herself—and karma—that if she ever ran into any of her former classmates from Emerson whom she had mistreated as a teenager, she would apologize and do whatever it took to make amends. It figured that when fate finally threw one of her former victims into her path, it would start with the biggie.

So why hadn't she tried to make amends on Saturday? Why hadn't she apologized? Why had she instead let him think she was still the same vain, shallow, snotty girl she'd been in high school?

Okay, here was a second chance to put things to right, she told herself. Even if she wasn't sure how to make up for her past behavior, the least she could do was apologize.

"Actually, Lucy, why don't you show him into the office instead?"

Lucy's surprise was obvious. Ava never let anyone but employees see the working parts of the boutique. The public areas of the store were plush and opulent, furnished with gilded Louis Quatorze tables and velvet upholstered chairs, baroque chandeliers and Aubusson carpets—reproductions, of course, but all designed to promote the same air of sumptuousness the designer clothes afforded her clients. The back rooms were functional and basic. Her office was small and cluttered, the computer and printer the only things that could be called state-of-the-art. The floor was concrete, the walls were cinder block, the ceiling was foam board and nothing was pretty.

Lucy's head disappeared from the door, but

her voice trailed behind her. "You can go back to the office. It's right through there."

Ava swiped a hand over the form-fitting jaguar-print dress she had donned that morning—something new from Yves Saint Laurent she'd wanted to test for comfort and wearability. She had just tucked a stray strand of auburn back into her French twist when Peyton appeared in the doorway, dwarfing the already tiny space.

He looked even better than he had the last time she saw him. His hair was deliciously wind tossed, and his whiskey-colored eyes were clearer. He'd substituted the rumpled suit of Saturday morning with faded jeans and a weathered leather jacket that hung open over a baggy chocolate-brown sweater. Battered hiking boots replaced the businesslike loafers.

He looked more like he had in high school. At least, the times in high school when she'd run into him outside of Emerson. Even in his school uniform, though, Peyton had managed to look different from the other boys. His shirttail had always hung out, his shoes had always been scuffed, his necktie had never been snug.

Back then, she'd thought he was just a big slob. But now she suspected he'd deliberately cultivated his look to differentiate himself from the other kids at Emerson. Nowadays, she didn't blame him.

He said nothing at first, only gazed at her the way he had on Saturday, as if he couldn't quite believe she was real. Gradually he relaxed, and even went so far as to lean against the doorjamb and shove his hands into the pockets of his jeans. Somehow, though, Ava sensed he was striving for a nonchalance he didn't really feel.

"Hi," he finally said.

"Hi yourself."

She tried to be as detached as he was, but she felt the same way she had Saturday—as if she were in high school again. As if she needed to shoulder the mantle of rich bitch ice princess to protect herself from the barbs she knew would be forthcoming. She was horrified by the thought—horrified that the girl she used to be might still be lurking somewhere inside her. She never wanted to be that person again. She never *would* be that person again. In spite of that, something about Peyton made the haughty teenager bubble up inside her.

Silence descended for an awkward moment. Then Peyton said, "You surprised me, being here. I came into the shop to see if anyone working knew where I could find you. I didn't expect you to actually be here."

Because he didn't think she actually *worked* here, Ava recalled, battling the defensiveness again. She told herself not to let his comment get to her and reminded herself to make amends. The best way to do that was to be the person she was now, not the person she used to be.

"I'm here more often than you might think," she said—sidestepping the truth again.

Then again, one couldn't exactly hurry the appeasement of karma. It was one thing to make amends for past behaviors. It was another to spill her guts to Peyton about everything that happened to her family and admit how she'd ended up in the same position he'd been in in high school, and now she was really, really sorry for how she had behaved all those years. That wasn't really necessary, was it? To go into all that detail? A woman was entitled to some secrets. And Ava wasn't sure she could bear Peyton's smug satisfaction after he learned about it. Or, worse, if he displayed the same kind of fake pity so many of her former so-called friends did.

Oh, Ava, they would say whenever she ran into them. *Has your poor father gotten out of prison yet? No? Darling, how do you stand the humiliation? We must meet for lunch sometime, get you out of that dreary store where you have to work your fingers to the bone. I'll call you.*

No calls ever came, of course. Not that Ava wanted them to. And their comments didn't bother her, because she didn't care about those people anymore. But coming from Peyton… For some reason, she suspected such comments would bother her a lot.

So she stalled. "We're supposed to be receiving a couple of evening gowns from Givenchy today, and I wanted to look them over before they went out on the floor." All of which was true, she hastened to reassure herself. She just didn't mention that she would have also been at the store if they were expecting a shipment of bubble wrap. She put in more hours at Talk of the Town than her two full-timers did combined.

"Then I guess I was lucky I came in today," he said, looking a little anxious. Sounding a little anxious.

"What made you come in?" she asked. "I thought you were going to be all booked up with Henry Higginses and millionaire matchmakers while you were in town."

He grinned halfheartedly and shifted his weight from one foot to the other. Both actions were probably intended to make him look comfortable, but neither really did.

"Yeah… Well… Actually…" He took a breath, released it slowly and tried again. "Actually, that's kind of why I'm here."

He gestured toward the only other chair in the office and asked, "Mind if I sit down?"

"Of course not," she replied. Even though she did kind of mind, because doing that would bring him closer, and then she would be the one trying to look comfortable when she felt anything but.

He folded himself into the other chair and continued to look uneasy. She waited for him to say something, but he only looked around the office, his gaze falling first on the Year in Fashion calendar on the wall—for April, it was Pierre Cardin—then on the fat issues of *Vogue, Elle* and *Marie Claire* that lined the top shelf of her desk, then lower, on the stack of catalogs sitting next to the employee schedule she'd been working on, and then—

Oh, dear. The employee schedule, which had her name and hours prominently at the top. Hastily, she scooped up the catalogs and laid them atop the schedule, tossing her pencil onto both.

He finally returned his gaze to her face. "The Henry Higgins didn't work out."

"What happened?"

His gaze skittered away again. "He told me I had to stop swearing and clean up my language."

Ava bit her lip to keep from smiling, since, to Peyton, this was clearly an insurmountable problem. "Well, if you're going to be dealing with two sweet little old ladies from Mississippi who are in their eighties and wear hats and white gloves, that's probably good advice."

"Yeah, but the Montgomery sisters are like

five states away. They can't hear me swearing in Chicago."

"But if it's a habit, now is a good time to start breaking it, since—"

"Dammit, Ava, I can stop swearing anytime I want to."

"Oh, really?" she said mildly.

"Hell, yes."

"I see."

"And you should have seen the suits he tried to put me into," Peyton added.

"Well, suits are part and parcel for businesspeople," Ava pointed out, "especially those in your position. You were wearing a suit at Basilio's the other night. What's the sudden problem with suits?"

"The problem wasn't suits. It was the suits this guy wanted to put me into."

She waited for him to explain, and when he didn't, asked, "Could you be a little more specific?"

He frowned. "One was purple. Oh, excuse me," he quickly corrected himself. "I mean *eggplant.* The other was the same color green the guys on the team used to spew after getting bodychecked too hard."

Ava thought for a minute, then said, "Loden, I think, is the color you're looking for."

"Yeah. That's it."

"Those are both very fashionable colors," she said. "Especially for younger guys like you. Sounds to me like Henry knew his stuff."

Peyton shook his head. "Suits should never be anything except gray, brown or black. Not slate, not espresso, not ebony," he added in a voice that indicated he'd already had this conversation with Henry Higgins. "Gray. Brown. Black. Maybe, in certain situations, navy blue. Not midnight," he said when she opened her mouth to comment. "Navy blue. They sure as hell shouldn't be purple or puke-green."

Ava closed her mouth.

"And don't get me started on the etiquette lessons the guy said I had to take," Peyton continued. "Or all that crap about comportment. Whatever the hell that is. He even tried to tell me what I can and can't eat in a restaurant."

"Peyton, all of those things are important when

it comes to dealing with people in professional situations. Especially when you're conducting business with people who do it old school, the way it sounds like the Montgomery sisters do."

He frowned. "Ava, I didn't get where I am today by studying etiquette books or comporting myself—whatever the hell that is. I did it by knowing what I want and going after it."

"And that's obviously worked in the past," she agreed. "But you admitted yourself that you'll have to operate differently with the Montgomerys. That means using a new rule book."

"I like my rule book just fine."

"Then do your takeover your way."

Why was he here? she asked herself again. This was an odd conversation to be having with him. Still, they were getting along. Kind of. Maybe she should just go with the flow.

He growled something unintelligible under his breath, but if she had to wager a guess, she'd bet it was more of that profanity he was supposed to be keeping under wraps.

His voice gentled some. "All I'm saying is that this guy doesn't know me from Adam, and he has no idea what's going to work for me and what isn't. I need to work with someone who can, you know, smooth my rough edges without sawing them off."

Okay, she was starting to understand. He wanted to see if she could recommend another stylist for him. Since she owned a shop like Talk of the Town, he figured she had connections in the business that might help him out.

"There are several stylists in Chicago who are very good," she said. "Some of them bring their clients to me." She reached for a binder filled with business cards she'd collected over the years. "Just give me a minute to find someone whose personality jibes with yours."

Ha. As if. There wasn't a human being alive whose personality jibed with Peyton's. Peyton was too larger-than-life. The best she could hope for was to find someone who wasn't easily intimidated. Hmm…maybe that guy who worked with the Bears before their last Super Bowl appearance. He'd had to have a couple of teeth replaced, but still…

Peyton placed his hand over hers before she

had a chance to open the binder. She tried to ignore the ruffle of butterflies in her midsection. Ha. As if.

His voice seemed to come from a very great distance when he spoke again. "No, Ava, you don't understand. Anyone you recommend is going to be in the same boat as Henry Higgins. They won't know me. They won't have any idea what to do with me."

She said nothing for a moment, only gazed at his hand covering hers, noting how it was twice the size of her own, how much rougher and darker, how his nails were blunt and square alongside her smooth, taupe-lacquered ovals. Their hands were so different from each other. So why did they fit together so well? Why did his touch feel so…right?

Reluctantly, she pulled her hand from beneath his and moved it to her lap. "Then why are you…"

The moment her gaze connected with his again, she began to understand. Surely, he wasn't suggesting… There was no way he… It was ludicrous to even think… He couldn't want *her* to be his stylist.

Could he?

She was his lifelong nemesis. He'd said so himself. Not to her face, but to a friend of his. She'd overhead the two of them talking as they came out of the boys' restroom near her locker at Emerson. The seniors had been studying *Romeo and Juliet,* and she'd heard him say that the Montagues and Capulets had nothing on the Mosses and Brenners. He'd told his friend that he and Ava would be enemies forever. Then he'd ordered a plague on her house.

Very carefully, she asked, "Peyton, why exactly are you here?"

He leaned forward in the chair, hooking his hands together between his legs. His gaze never leaving hers, he said, "Exactly? I'm here because I didn't know where else to go. There aren't many people left in this city who remember me—"

Oh, she sincerely doubted that.

"And there are even fewer I care about seeing."

That she could definitely believe.

"And I'm not supposed to go back to San Francisco until I'm, um—" he made a restless gesture with his hand, as if he were literally groping for the right word "—until I'm fit for the right kind of society."

When Ava said nothing in response—because she honestly had no idea what to say—he expelled a restless breath and leaned back in the chair again.

Finally, point-blank, he said, "Ava, I want you to be my Henrietta Higgins."

Peyton told himself he shouldn't be surprised by Ava's deer-in-the-headlights reaction. He'd had a similar one when the idea popped into his head as he was escaping Henry Higgins's office the previous afternoon. But there was no way he could have kept working with that guy, and something told him anyone else was going to be just as bad or worse.

How was someone going to turn him from a sow's ear into a silk purse if they didn't even know how he'd become a sow's ear in the first place? He'd never be a silk purse anyway. He needed to work with someone who understood that the best they could hope for would be to turn him into something in between. Like a… hmm…like maybe a cotton pigskin. Yeah, that's it. Like a denim football. He could do that. He could go from a sow's ear to a denim football. But he was still going to need help getting there. And it was going to have to be from someone who not only knew how to look and act in society, but who knew him and his limitations.

And who knew his limitations better than Ava? Who understood society better than Ava? Maybe she didn't like him. Maybe he didn't like her. But he knew her. And she knew him. That was more than he could say for all the Henry Higginses in the world. He and Ava had worked together once, in spite of their differences—they'd actually pulled off an A-minus on that World Civ project in high school. So why couldn't they work together as adults? Hell, adults should be even better at putting aside their differences, right? Peyton worked with people he didn't like all the time.

The tension between him and Ava on Saturday morning had probably just been a result of their shock at seeing each other again. Probably. Hey, they were being civil to each other now, weren't they? Or at least they had been. Before he dropped the Henrietta Higgins bombshell and Ava went all catatonic on him.

"So what do you say, Ava?" he asked in an effort to get the conversation rolling again. "Think you could help me out here?"

"I, ah..." she nonanswered.

"I mean, this sort of thing is right up your alley, right? Even if you didn't own a store that deals with, you know, fashion and stuff." *Fashion and stuff?* Could he sound more like an adolescent? "You know all about how people are supposed to dress and act in social situations."

"Yes, but..."

"And you know me well enough to not to dress me in purple."

"Well, that's certainly true, but..."

"And you'd talk to me the right way. Like you wouldn't say—" He adopted what he thought was a damned good impression of the man who had tried to dress him in purple. "'Mr. Moss, would you be ever so kind as to cease usage of the vulgar sort of language we decided earlier might be a detriment to your reception by the ladies whom you are doing your best to impress.' You'd just say, 'Peyton, the Montgomerys are going to wash your mouth out with soap if you don't stop dropping the F-bomb.' And just like that, I'd know what the hell you were talking about, and I'd do it right away."

This time, Ava only arched an eyebrow in what could have been amusement or censure… or something else he probably didn't want to identify.

"Okay, so maybe I wouldn't do it right away," he qualified. "But at least I would know what you were talking about, and we could come to some sort of compromise."

The eyebrow lowered, but the edge of her mouth twitched a little. Even though he wasn't sure whether it was twitching up or down, Peyton decided to be optimistic. At least she hadn't thrown anything at him.

"I just mean," he said, "that you…that I…that we…" He blew out an irritated breath, sat up straighter, and looked her straight in the eye. "Look, Ava, I know we were never the best of friends…" *Even if we were—for one night, anyway—lovers,* he couldn't help thinking. Hoping she wasn't thinking that, too. Figuring she probably was. Not sure how he felt about any of it. "But I obviously need help with this new and improved me, and I'm not going to get it from some total stranger. I don't know anyone here who could help me except you. Because you're the only one here who knows me."

"I *did* know you," she corrected him. "When we were in high school. Neither of us is the person we were then."

There was something in her voice that made Peyton hesitate. Although it was true that in a lot of ways he wasn't the person he'd been in high school, Ava obviously still was. Maybe the adult wasn't quite as snotty, vain or superficial as the girl had been, but she could still put a guy in his place. She was still classy. She was still beautiful. She was still out of his league. Hell, she hadn't changed at all.

"So will you do it?" he asked, deliberately not giving her time to think it over.

She thought it over anyway. Dammit. Her gaze never left his, but he could almost hear the crackling of her brain synapses as she connected all the dots and came to her conclusions. He was relieved when she finally smiled.

Until she asked, "How much does the position pay?"

His mouth fell open. "Pay?"

She nodded. "Pay. Surely you were paying your previous stylist."

"Well, yeah, but that was his job."

She shrugged. "And your point would be?"

He didn't know what his point was. He'd just figured Ava would help him out. He hadn't planned on her being mercenary about it.

Wow. She really hadn't changed since high school.

"Fine," he said coolly. "I'll pay you what I was paying him." He named the figure, one that was way too high to pay anyone for telling people how to dress and talk and eat.

Ava shook her head. "No, you'll have to do better than that."

"What?"

"Peyton, if you want to make use of my expertise in this matter, then I expect to be compensated accordingly."

Of course she did. Ava Brenner never did anything unless she was compensated.

"Fine," he said again. "How much do you charge for your expertise?"

She thought for another minute, then quoted a figure fifty percent higher than what he had offered.

"You're nuts," he told her. "You could build the Taj Mahal for that."

She said nothing.

He offered her 10 percent more.

She said nothing.

He offered her 25 percent more.

She tilted her head to one side.

He offered her 40 percent more.

"All right," she said with a satisfied smile.

"Great," he muttered.

"Well, I didn't want to be unreasonable."

This time Peyton was the one who said nothing. But he suddenly realized it wasn't because he was irritated with their lopsided bargaining—as if Ava was any kind of bargain. It was because it felt kind of good to be sparring with her again. He remembered now how, despite the antagonism of their exchanges in high school, he'd always come away from them feeling weirdly energized and satisfied. Although he still sparred with plenty of people these days, none ever left him feeling the way he'd felt taking on Ava.

"But Peyton, you'll have to do things my way," she said, pulling him out of his musing.

Peyton hated it when people told him they had to do things any way other than his own. He waited for the resentment and hostility that normally came along with such demands to coil inside him. Instead, he felt strangely elated.

"All right," he conceded. "We'll do this your way."

She grinned. He told himself it was smugly. But damned if she didn't look kind of happy to have taken on the task, too.

Four

Scarcely an hour after Ava agreed to be Peyton's makeover artist, she sat across from him at a table in a State Street restaurant. He'd asked her if they could get started right away, since he was eager to get on with his corporate takeover and had already lost a week to his previous stylist. And since—Hey, Ava, would ya look at that?—it was coming up on noon anyway, lunch sounded like a really good idea. After ensuring that one of her morning clerks would be able to pull an afternoon shift, too, Ava had agreed.

As surprised as she'd been by his request to help him out, she was even more surprised to realize she was happy to be doing it. Though not because he was paying her, since the figure she'd quoted him would barely cover the cost of the two additional salesclerks she'd need at Talk of the Town to cover for her. The strange happiness, she was certain, stemmed from the fact that she would finally be able to make amends for the way she had treated him in high school. It was that, and nothing more, that caused the funny buzz of delight that hummed inside her.

Anyway, what difference did it make? The point was that she would be helping Peyton become a gentleman, thereby ensuring he added to his already enormous financial empire. The point was that she would be performing enough good deeds over the next week or so to counter a lot of the mean things she'd said and done to him in high school. And the point was that, by helping him this way, she wouldn't have to bare her soul about the specifics of her current lifestyle. Specifically, she wouldn't have to tell him how she didn't have any style in her life, save what she was surrounded by at work every day.

What would telling Peyton about what happened to her family sixteen years ago accomplish? It wouldn't change anything. Why shouldn't she just do this nice thing for him and make some small amends for her past? No harm, no foul. They could complete the mission, job well done, then he could be on his way back to the West Coast none the wiser.

Yeah. That's the ticket.

She sighed inwardly as she looked at Peyton. Not because of how handsome he was sitting there looking at the menu—though he was certainly handsome sitting there looking at the menu—but because he was slumped forward with one elbow on the table, his chin settled in his hand. He had also preceded her to the table and seated himself without a second thought for her, then snatched up the menu as if it he hadn't eaten in a week. Combined, the actions gave her some small inkling of what his previous Henry Higgins had been up against.

"Peyton," she said quietly.

His gaze never left the menu. "Yeah?"

She said nothing until he looked up at her. She hoped he would realize she was setting an example for him to follow when she straightened in her chair and plucked the menu delicately from the table, laying her other hand in her lap.

He changed his posture not at all. "What is it?"

She threw her shoulders back and sat up even straighter.

"What?" he repeated, more irritably this time.

Fine. If he was going to behave like a child, she'd treat him like a child. "Sit up straight."

He looked confused. "Say what?"

"Sit up straight."

He narrowed his eyes and opened his mouth as if he were going to object, but she arched one eyebrow meaningfully and he closed his mouth again. To his credit, he also straightened in his chair and leaned against its back. She could tell he wasn't happy about completing the action. But he did complete it.

"Take your elbow off the table," she further instructed.

He frowned at her, but did as she said.

Satisfied she had his attention—maybe a little more than she wanted—she continued with her lesson. "Also, when you're in a restaurant with a woman and the host is taking you to your table, you should always invite her to walk ahead of you and follow her so that—"

"But how will she know where she's going if she's walking ahead of me?" he interrupted.

Ava maintained her calm, teacherly persona. "This may come as a surprise to you, Peyton, but women can generally follow a restaurant host to a table every bit as well as a man can. Furthermore," she hurried on when he opened his mouth to object again, "when the two of you arrive at the table, if the host doesn't direct her to a chair and pull it out for her, then you need to do that."

"But I thought you women hated it when men pull out a chair for you, or open the door for you, or do anything else for you."

"Some women would prefer to do those things themselves, true, but not all women. Society has moved past a time when that kind of thing was viewed as sexist, and now it's simply a matter of common—"

"Since when?" he barked. Interrupting her. Again. "The last time I opened a door for a woman, she about cleaned my clock for it."

Ava managed to maintain her composure. "And when was that?"

He thought for a minute. "Actually, I think it was you who did that. I was on my way out of chemistry and you were on your way in."

Ava remembered the episode well. "The reason I wanted to clean your clock wasn't because you held the door open for me. It was because you and Tom Sellinger made woofing sounds as I walked through it."

Instead of looking chagrined, Peyton grinned. "Oh, yeah. I forgot that part."

"Anyway," she continued, "these days it's a matter of common courtesy to open a door for someone—male or female—and to pull out a woman's chair for her. But you're right that some women prefer to do that themselves. You'll know a woman who does by the way she chooses a chair when she arrives at the table and immediately pulls it out for herself. That's a good indication that you don't have to do it for her."

"Gotcha," he said. Still grinning. Damn him.

"But from what you've told me about the

Misses Montgomery," Ava said, "they'll expect you to extend the courtesy to them."

"Yeah, okay," he muttered. "I guess you have a point."

"Don't mutter," she said.

He narrowed his eyes at her again. But his voice was much clearer when he said, "Fine. The next time I'm in a restaurant with a woman, I'll let her go first and watch for clues. Anything else?"

"Oh, yes," Ava assured him enthusiastically. "We've only just begun. Once you sit down, let her open her menu first." When he started to ask another question that would doubtless be more about when women had changed their minds about this sort of thing—as if women had ever stopped having the prerogative to change their minds about whatever they damned well pleased—she continued, "And when you're looking at your menu, it's nice to make conversation over the choices. Don't just sit there staring at it until you make a decision. Ask your companion what she thinks looks good, too. If you're in a restaurant where you've eaten before, you might even make suggestions about dishes you like."

He considered her for another moment, then asked, "You're not going to make me order for you, are you? I hate that."

"*I* won't make you order for *me,*" she said. "But some women like for men to do that."

"Well, how the hell will I know if they want me to or not?"

Ava cleared her throat discreetly. He looked at her as if he had no idea why. She stood her silent ground. He replayed what he had just said, then rolled his eyes.

"Fine. How…will I know?" he enunciated clearly, pausing over the spot where the profanity had been.

"You'll know because she'll tell you what she's planning to have, and when your waiter approaches, you'll look at her, and she'll look back at you and not say anything. If she looks at the waiter and says she'll start with the crab bisque and then moves on to the salad course, you'll know she's going to order for herself."

"So what do you think the Montgomerys will do?"

"I have no idea."

"Dammit, Ava, I—"

She arched her eyebrow again. He growled his discontent.

"I hate this," he finally hissed. "I hate having to act like someone I'm not."

Ava disagreed that he was being forced to act like someone he wasn't, since she was confident that somewhere deep inside he did have the potential to be a gentleman. In spite of that, she told him, "I know you do. And after your takeover of the Montgomerys' company is finished, if you want to go back to your reprobate ways, no one will stop you. Until then, if you want your takeover to be successful, you're going to have to do what I tell you."

He blew out an exasperated sound and grumbled another ripe obscenity. So Ava snapped her menu shut and stood, collecting her purse from the back of her chair as she went.

"Hey!" he said as he rose, too, following her. "Where the hell do you think you're going? You said you would help me out."

She never broke stride. "Not if you won't even try. I have better things to do with my afternoon than sit here watching you sulk and listening to you swear."

"Yeah, I guess you could get a crapload of shopping done this afternoon, couldn't you?" he replied. "Then you could hit that restaurant where you know everyone's name. Some guy there will pull out your chair for you and do all the ordering. And I bet he never swears."

She halted and spun around to face him. "You know, Peyton, I'm not sure you *are* fit for polite society. Go ahead and bulldoze your way over two nice old ladies. You were always much better at that than you were asking for something politely."

Why had she thought this could work? Just because the two of them had managed to be civil to each other for ten minutes in her office? Yeah, right. Ten minutes was about the longest the two of them had ever been able to be in each other's presence before the bombs began to drop.

Well, except for that night at her parents' house, she remembered. Then again, that had been pretty explosive, too…

"Excuse me," she said as civilly as she could

before turning her back on him again and making her way toward the exit.

She took two steps before he caught her by the arm and spun her around. She was tempted to take advantage of the momentum to slam her purse into his shoulder, but one of them had to be a grown-up. And she was barely managing to do that herself.

She steeled herself for another round of combat, but he only said softly, sincerely, “I’m sorry.”

She relaxed. Some. “I forgive you.”

“Will you come back to the table? Please?”

She knew the apology hadn’t come easily for him. His use of the word *please* had probably been even harder. He was trying. Maybe the two of them would always be like fire and ice, but he was making an effort. It would be small of her not to give it—not to give him—another chance.

“Okay,” she said. “But, Peyton…” She deliberately left the statement unfinished. She’d made clear her terms already.

“I know,” he said. “I understand. And I promise I’ll do what you tell me to do. I promise to be what you want me to be.”

Well, Ava doubted that. Certainly Peyton would be able to do and say the things she told him to do and say. But be what she wanted him to be? That was never going to happen. He would never be forgiving of the way she had treated him in high school. He would never be able to see her as anything other than the queen bee she'd been then. He would never be her friend. Not that she blamed him for any of those things. The best she could hope for was that he would, after this, have better memories of her to replace the ugly ones. If nothing else, maybe, in the future, when—if—he thought of her, it would be with a little less acrimony.

And, hey, that wasn't terrible, right?

"Let's start over," she said.

He nodded. "Okay."

She was talking about the afternoon, of course. But she couldn't help thinking how nice it would be if they could turn back the clock a couple of decades and start over there, too.

The last time Peyton was in a tailor's shop—in fact, the only time Peyton was in a tailor's shop—it had been a cut-rate establishment in his old neighborhood that had catered to low-budget weddings and proms. Which was why he'd been there in the first place, to rent a tux for Emerson's prom. The place had been nothing like the mahogany-paneled, Persian-carpeted wonder in which he now stood. He always bought his clothes off the rack and wore whatever he yanked out of the closet. If the occasion was formal, there was the tux he'd bought at a warehouse sale not long after he graduated from college. His girlfriend at the time had dragged him there, and she'd deemed it a vintage De la Renta—whatever the hell that was—that would remain timeless forever. It had cost him forty bucks, which he'd figured was a pretty good deal for timelessness.

Ava, evidently, had other ideas. All it had taken was one look at the dozen articles of clothing he'd brought with him, and she'd concluded his entire wardrobe needed revamping. Sure, she'd been tactful enough to use phrases like *a little out-of-date* and *not the best fitting* and *lower tier*. The end result was the same. She'd hated everything he brought with him. And when he'd told her about the vintage De la Renta back in San Francisco and how he'd worn it as recently as a month ago, she'd looked as though she wanted to lose her breakfast.

Now she stood beside him in front of the tailor's mirror, and Peyton studied her reflection instead of his own—all three panels of it. He still couldn't get over how beautiful she was. The clingy leopard-print dress she'd worn the day before had been replaced by more casual attire today, a pair of baggy tan trousers and a creamy sweater made of some soft fuzzy stuff that didn't cling at all. She'd left her hair down but still had it pulled back in a clip at her nape. He wondered what it took—besides going to bed—to make her wear it loose, the way it had been Saturday morning. Then again, as reasons went for a woman wearing her hair loose, going to bed was a pretty good one.

"Show him something formal in Givenchy," she said, speaking to the tailor. "And bring him some suits from Hugo Boss. Darks. Maybe something with a small pinstripe. Nothing too reckless."

The tailor was old enough to be Peyton's grandfather, but at least his suit wasn't purple. On the contrary, it was a sedate dark gray that was, even to Peyton's untrained eye, impeccably cut. He had a tape measure around his neck, little black glasses perched on his nose and a tuft of white hair encircling his head from one ear to the other. His name was the very no-nonsense Mr. Endicott.

"Excellent choices, Miss Brenner," Mr. Endicott said before scurrying off to find whatever it was she had asked him to bring.

Ava turned her attention to Peyton, studying his reflection as he was hers. She smiled reassuringly. "Hugo Boss is a favorite of men in your position," she said. "He's like the perfect designer for high-powered executives. At least, the ones who don't want to wear eggplant, loden or espresso."

Peyton started to correct her about the high-powered-executive thing, then remembered that he was, in fact, a high-powered executive.

Funny, but he hadn't felt like one since coming back to Chicago.

"I promise he won't bring you anything in purple or puke-green," she clarified when he didn't reply. "He's one of the most conservative tailors in Chicago."

Peyton nodded, but still said nothing. A weird development, since he'd never been at a loss for words around Ava before. He'd said a lot of things to her when they were in high school that he shouldn't have. Even if she'd been vain, snotty and shallow, she hadn't deserved some of the treatment she'd received from him. There were a couple of times in particular that he maybe, possibly, perhaps should apologize for…

"It's not that your other clothes are bad," she added, evidently mistaking his silence as irritation. "Like I said, they just need a little, um, updating."

She was trying hard not to say anything that might create tension between them. And the two of them had gotten along surprisingly well all morning. They'd been stilted and formal and in no way comfortable with each other, but they'd gotten along.

"Look, Ava, I'm not going to jump down your throat for telling me I'm not fashionable," he said. "I know I'm not. I'm doing this because I'm about to enter a sphere of the business world I've never moved in before, one that has expectations I'll have to abide by." He shrugged. "But I have to learn what they are. That's why you're here. I won't bite your head off if you tell me what I'm doing wrong."

She arched that eyebrow at him again, the way she had the day before at the restaurant, when he'd bitten her head off for telling him what he was doing wrong.

"Anymore," he amended. "I won't bite your head off anymore."

The eyebrow went back down, and she smiled. It wasn't a big smile, but it was a start. If nothing else, it told him she was willing to keep reminding him, as long as he was willing to remember he'd reminded her to do it.

The tailor returned with a trio of suits and a single tuxedo, and Peyton blew out a silent breath of relief that none of them could be called anything but *dark.* The man then helped Peyton out of his leather jacket and gestured for him to shed the dark blue sweater beneath it. When he stood in his white V-neck T-shirt and jeans, the tailor helped him on with the first suit jacket, made some murmuring sounds, whipped the tape measure from around his neck, and began to measure Peyton's arms, shoulders and back.

"Now the trousers," the man said.

Peyton looked at Ava in the mirror.

"I think it's okay if you go in the fitting room for that," she said diplomatically.

Right. Fitting room. He knew that. At least, he knew that *now.*

When he returned some minutes later wearing what he had to admit was a faultless charcoal pinstripe over a crisp white dress shirt the tailor had also found for him, Ava had her back to him, inspecting two neckties she had picked up in his absence.

"So…what do you think?" he asked.

As he approached her, he tried to look more comfortable than he felt. Though his discomfort wasn't due to the fact that he was wearing a garment with a price tag higher than that of any of the cars he'd owned in his youth. It was because he was worried Ava still wouldn't approve of him, even dressed in the exorbitant plumage of her tribe.

His fear was compounded when she spun around smiling, only to have her smile immediately fall. Dammit. She still didn't like him. No, he corrected himself—she didn't like what he was wearing. Big difference. He didn't care if she didn't like him. He didn't. He only needed for her to approve of his appearance. Which she obviously didn't.

"Wow," she said.

Oh. Okay. So maybe she did approve.

"You look…" She drew in a soft breath and expelled it. "Wow."

Something hot and fizzy zipped through his midsection at her reaction. It was a familiar sensation, but one he hadn't felt for a long time. More than fifteen years, in fact. It was the same sensation he'd felt one time when Ava looked at him from across their shared classroom at

Emerson. For a split second, she hadn't registered that it was Peyton she was looking at, and her smile had been dreamy and wistful. In that minuscule stretch of time, she had looked at him as if he were something worth looking at, and it had made him feel as if nothing in his life would ever go wrong again.

Somehow, right now, he had that feeling again.

"So you like it?" he asked.

"Very much," she said. Dreamily. Wistfully. And heat whipped through his belly again. She finally seemed to remember where she was and what she was supposed to be doing, because she looked down at the lengths of silk in her hand. He couldn't help thinking she sounded a little flustered when she said, "But you, ah, you need a tie."

She took a few steps toward him, stopped for some reason, then completed a few more that brought her within touching distance. Instead of closing the gap, though, she held up the two neckties, one in each hand.

"I hope you don't mind," she said, "but I'm of the opinion that the necktie is where a man truly shows his personality. The suit can be as conservative as they come, but the tie can be a little more playful and interesting." She hesitated. "Provided that fits the character of the man."

He wanted to ask if she actually thought he was playful, never mind interesting, but said nothing. Mostly because he had noted two spots of pink coloring her cheeks and had become fascinated by them. Was she blushing, or was the heat in the store just set too high? Then he realized it was actually kind of cool in there. Which meant she must be—

"If you don't like these, I can look for something different," she told him, taking another step that still didn't bring her as close as he would have liked. "But these two made me think of you."

Peyton forced himself to look at the ties. One was splashed with amorphous shapes in a half dozen colors, and the other looked like a watercolor rendition of a tropical rain forest. He was surprised to discover he liked them. The colors were bold without being obnoxious, and the patterns were masculine without being aggressive.

The fact that Ava said they reminded her of him made him feel strangely flattered.

"I'll just look for something different then," she said when he didn't reply, once again misinterpreting his silence as disapproval. "There were some nice striped ones you might like better." She started to turn away.

"No, Ava, wait."

In one stride, he covered the distance between them and curled his fingers around her arm, spinning her gently around to face him. Her eyes were wide with surprise, her mouth slightly open. And God help him, all he wanted was to keep tugging her forward until he could cover her mouth with his and wreak havoc on them both.

"I, uh, I like them," he said, shoving aside his errant thoughts.

Once again, he forced himself to look at the ties. But all he saw was the elegant fingers holding them, her nails perfect ovals of red. That night at her parents' house, her nails had been perfect ovals of pink. He'd thought the color then was so much more innocent-looking than Ava was. Until the two of them finally came together, and he realized she wasn't as experienced as he thought, that he was the first guy to—

"Let's try that one," he said, not sure which tie he was talking about.

"Which one?"

"The one on the right," he managed.

"My right or your right?"

He stifled the frustrated obscenity hovering at the back of his throat. "Yours."

She held up the tie with the unstructured forms and smiled. "That was my favorite, too."

Great.

Before he realized what she was planning, she stepped forward and looped the tie around his neck, turning up the collar of his shirt to thread it underneath. He was assailed by a soft, floral scent that did nothing to dispel the sixteen-year-old memories still dancing in his head, and the flutter of her fingers as she wrapped the length of silk around itself jacked his pulse rate higher. In an effort to keep his sanity, he closed his eyes and began to list in alphabetical order all the microbreweries he had visited on his travels. Thankfully, by the time he came to Zywiec in Poland, she was pulling the knot snug at his throat.

"There," she said, sounding a little breathless herself. "That should, ah, do it."

He did his best to ignore the last two words and the fact that she had stumbled over them. She couldn't be thinking about the same thing he was.

"Thanks," he muttered, the word sounding in no way grateful.

"You're welcome," she muttered back, the sentiment sounding in no way generous.

When he opened his eyes, he saw Ava glaring at him. Worse, he knew he was glaring at her, too. Before either of them could say anything that might make the situation worse, he went back to the mirror. Mr. Endicott took that as his cue to start with the measuring and adjusting again. He made a few notations on a pad of paper, struck a few marks on the garment with a piece of chalk, stuck a few pins into other places and told Peyton to go try on the next suit.

When he returned in that one, Ava was near

the mirror draping a few more neckties onto a wooden valet. Upon his approach, she hurriedly finished, then strode to nearly the other side of the room. Jeez, it was as though anytime the two of them spent more than an hour in each other's presence, a switch flipped somewhere that sent a disharmony ray shooting over them. What the hell was up with that?

This time Peyton tied his own damned tie—though not with the expertise Ava had—then turned for her approval. Only to see her still riffling through some neckties on a table that she'd probably already riffled through.

He cleared his throat to get her attention.

She continued her necktie hunt.

He turned back to the tailor. "This one is fine, too."

Out came the tape measure and chalk again. The ritual was performed twice more—including Peyton's futile efforts to win Ava's attention—until even the tuxedo was fitted. Only when he was stepping down from the platform in that extraformal monkey suit did Ava look up at him again. Only this time, she didn't look away. This time, her gaze swept him from the top of his head to the tips of his shoes and back.

He held his breath, waiting to see if she would smile.

She didn't. Instead she said, "I, um, I think that will do nicely." Before Peyton had a chance to say thanks, she added, "But you need a haircut."

All Peyton could think was, *Two steps forward, one step back.* What the hell. He'd take it.

"I'm guessing that's somewhere on our to-do list?" he asked.

She nodded. "This afternoon. I made an appointment for you at my salon. They're fabulous."

"Your *salon?*" he echoed distastefully. "What's wrong with a barbershop?"

"Nothing. If you're a dockworker."

"Ava, I've never set foot in a salon. A record I plan to keep."

"But it's unisex," she said, as if that made everything okay.

"I don't care if it's forbidden sex. Find me a good barber."

She opened her mouth to argue, but his unwillingness to bend on the matter must have shown in his expression. So she closed her mouth and said nothing. Not that that meant she would find him a barber. But at least they could bicker about it after they left the tailor's.

And why was he kind of looking forward to that?

When it became obvious that neither of them was going to say more, Peyton made his way back to Endicott, who led him back to the fitting room.

"Don't worry, Mr. Moss," the tailor said. "You're doing fine."

Peyton looked up at that. "What?"

"Miss Brenner," Endicott said as he continued to walk, speaking over his shoulder. "She likes the suits. She likes the tuxedo even more."

"How can you tell?"

The tailor simply grinned. "Don't worry," he repeated. "She likes you, too."

Peyton opened his mouth to reply, but no words emerged. Which was just as well, because Mr. Endicott continued walking, throwing up a hand to gesture him forward.

"Come along, Mr. Moss. I still need to pin those trousers."

Sure thing, Peyton thought. Just as soon as he pinned some thoughts back into his brain.

Five

After addressing Peyton's wardrobe and hair, ah, challenges, Ava turned his attention to the appreciation of life's finer things—art, music, theater. At least, that was where she was planning to turn his attention the morning after their sartorial adventures. No sooner did she rap lightly on the door of his hotel suite, however, than did she discover her plans were about to go awry.

"Sorry," he said by way of a greeting. "But we have to cancel this morning. I'm supposed to meet with the matchmaker. I forgot all about it yesterday when you and I made plans for this morning."

Ava told herself the reason for the sudden knot her stomach was because she was peeved at his last-minute canceling of their date. Ah, she meant *plans.* And she was peeved because they were *plans* she'd given herself the day off from work for when she might have saved herself some money instead of paying Lucy overtime. It had nothing to do with the fact that Peyton would be spending the morning with another woman.

Not that the other woman was, you know, *another woman,* since for her to be that, Ava would have to be the primary woman in his life, and of course that wasn't the case. Besides, the other woman he was seeing today was only a matchmaker. A matchmaker who would be setting him up with, well, *other women.* Women he would be seeing socially. Confidentially. Romantically.

The knot squeezed tighter. Because she was peeved, Ava reminded herself. Peeved that he was messing up their *plans.*

"Oh. Okay," she said, sounding troubled and unhappy, and in no way peeved.

"I'm really sorry," he apologized again. "When I checked my voice mail last night, there was a message from Caroline—she's the match-maker—reminding me. By then it was too late to call you, and you didn't answer your phone this morning."

He must have called while she was in the shower. "Well, you don't want to miss a meeting with her. I'm sure you and she have a lot to go over before you can launch your quest for Ms. Right."

"Actually, I've already met with her once. We're meeting today because she's rounded up some possible matches, and she wants me to look at their photos and go over their stats before she makes the actual introductions. Maybe we could just push things back to this afternoon?"

"Sure. No problem."

So what if Peyton was meeting with his match-maker? Ava asked herself. He was supposed to be doing that. Finding an appropriate woman was half the reason he was back in Chicago, and

Ava didn't even have to work with him on that part. She only had to make sure he was presentable to any woman he did meet.

She leaped on that realization. "But you know, Peyton, I'm not sure you're ready to meet any prospective dates just yet. We still have a lot of work to do to get you ready for that."

"How much more do we have to do?"

He'd actually come a long way in four days, Ava had to admit. And not just because of his stylish new wardrobe and excellent new haircut—which he had finally agreed to get at her salon, but not after much haggling. Haggling that, in hindsight, hadn't been all that unpleasant, especially when he seemed to be enjoying it as much as she did.

At any rate, his faded jeans and bulky sweater of the day before had made way for expensive dark-wash denim and a more fitted sweater in what she knew was espresso, but which she'd conceded to Peyton—after more surprisingly enjoyable haggling—was actually brown. His shorter hair had showcased the few threads of silver amid the black, something that gave him a definite executive aura—not to mention an added bit of sexiness. Ava's charcoal skirt and claret cashmere sweater set—both by Chanel—should have seemed dressy, but he made denim and cotton aristocratic to the point where she felt like the palace gardener. He was the kind of client that would make a matchmaker drool—never mind the effect he would have on his prospective matches. It was amazing what a little polish would do for a guy.

Then again, it wasn't always the clothes that made the man. What made Peyton Peyton was what was beneath the clothes. And that was something even teaching him about the finer things in life wouldn't change. Yes, he needed to learn to become a gentleman if he wanted to impress the sisters Montgomery and acquire their company. But there was too much roughneck in him to ever let the gentleman take over for very long.

It was a realization that should have made Ava even more peeved, since it suggested that everything she was doing to help him was pointless. Instead, it comforted her.

Remembering he'd asked her a question that needed a response, she said, "Well, I was kind of hoping to cover the arts this week. And we still need to fine-tune your restaurant etiquette. And we should—" She halted. There was no reason to make him think there was still tons more to do, since there really wasn't. For some reason, though, she found herself wishing there was still tons more to do. "Not a lot," she said. "There's not a lot."

Instead of looking pleased about that, he looked kind of, well, peeved.

"I should go," she told him. "What time do you think you'll be finished?"

"I don't know. Maybe I could call you when we're done?"

She nodded and started to turn away.

"Unless…"

She turned to face him. "Unless what?"

He looked a little uncomfortable. "Unless maybe…" He shoved his hands into the pockets of his jeans, a restless gesture. "Unless maybe you want to come with me?"

It was an odd request. For one thing, Caroline

the matchmaker would be curious—not to mention possibly peeved—if Peyton showed up with a woman. A woman who, by the way, Caroline had had no part in setting him up with, so she wouldn't be collecting a finder's fee. For another thing, why would Peyton want Ava with him when he considered a potentially life-changing decision?

As if he'd heard her unspoken question, he hurried on, "I mean, you might be able to give me some advice or something. I've never worked with a matchmaker before."

Oh, and she had? Jeez, she hadn't even had a date in more than a year. She was the last person who should be giving advice about matters of the heart. Not that Peyton needed to know any of that, but still.

"Please, Ava?" he asked, sounding as if he genuinely wanted her to come along. "You know what kind of woman I need to find. One who's just like—"

You. That was what he had been about to say. That was the word his lips had been about to form, the one hanging in the air between them, the one exiting his head and entering her own. Ava knew it as surely as she knew her own name.

After an almost imperceptible pause, he finished, "—Jackie Kennedy. I need to find a woman like Jackie Kennedy."

Oh, sure. As if there were *any* women in the world like Jackie Kennedy. How Peyton could have jumped from thinking about Ava to thinking about her was a mystery.

"Okay, I'll come with you," she said. She had no idea when she had made the decision to do so. And she was even more uncertain about why. What was really odd, though, was how, suddenly, somehow, she didn't feel quite as peeved as she had before.

The office of Attachments, Inc. had surprised Peyton on his first visit. He'd thought a matchmaker's office would be full of hearts and flowers, furnished with overblown Victorian furniture in a million different colors, with sappy chamber music playing over it all. Instead, the place was much like his own office in San Francisco, twenty stories above the city, with wide windows that offered panoramic views of Lake Michigan and Navy Pier, furnished in contemporary sleekness and soothing earth tones. The music was jazz, and the only plants were potted bamboo.

Caroline, too, had come as a surprise that first time. He'd expected a gingham-clad grandmother with a graying bun and glasses perched on her nose, but the woman who greeted him and Ava was a far cry from that. Yes, her hair was silver, but it hung loose and was stylishly cut, and her glasses were shoved atop her head. In place of gingham, she was wrapped in a snug, sapphire-colored dress and wearing mile-high heels that click-click-clicked on the tile floor as she approached them.

"Mr. Moss," she gushed when she came to a stop in front of him and extended her hand the way any high-powered business CEO would. "It is so nice to see you again." Her gushing ebbed considerably, however—in fact, the temperature seemed to drop fifty degrees—when she turned to Ava and said, "Now who are you?"

Before Ava had a chance to answer, Peyton replied, "She's my, ah, my assistant. Ava Brenner."

Caroline gave Ava a quick once-over and, evidently satisfied with his answer, immediately dismissed her. She turned to Peyton again. "Well, then. If you'd like to come back to my office, we can get down to business."

Confident the two of them would follow, she spun on her mile-high heels and click-click-clicked in the direction from which she'd come. Peyton turned to Ava and started to shrug, but stopped when he saw her expression. She looked kind of…peeved. Although that wasn't a word in his normal vocabulary, he couldn't think of any other adjective to describe her. She was looking at him as if he'd just insulted her. He backtracked the last few seconds in his brain, then remembered he'd introduced her as his assistant. Okay, so maybe that suggested she was his subordinate, but he was paying her to help him out, so that sort of made her an employee, and that kind of made her a subordinate. And what was the big deal anyway? Some of his best friends were subordinates.

Anyway, they didn't have time for another argument. So he only gestured after the hastily departing Caroline and asked, "Are you coming?"

"Do I have a choice?" she replied crisply.

He did shrug this time, hoping the gesture looked more sincere than it felt. "You could wait out here if you want."

For a moment, he thought she would take him up on that, and a weird panic rose in his belly. She wouldn't. He needed her to help him with this. He had no idea what kind of woman would be acceptable to his board of directors. Other than that she had to have all the qualities Ava had.

Caroline called back to them, and although Ava tensed even more, she turned in the direction of the matchmaker and began to march forward. Relief—and a strange kind of happiness—washed over Peyton as he followed. Because he needed her, he told himself. Or rather, he needed her *help.* That was why he was glad she hadn't stayed in the waiting room. It had nothing to do with how he just felt better having her at his side. The reason he felt better having her at his side was because, you know, she was helping him. Which he needed. Her help, he meant. Not her at his side.

Ah, hell. He was just happy—he meant *relieved*—that she was with him.

Caroline's office was a better reflection of her trade. The walls were painted the color of good red wine, and a wide Persian rug spanned a floor that had magically become hardwood. Her desk was actually kind of Victorian-looking, but it was tempered by the sleek city skyline in the windows behind her. On one wall hung certificates for various accomplishments, along with two degrees in psychology from Northwestern. Her bookshelf was populated less by books than by artifacts from world travels, but the books present were all about relationships and sexuality.

Instead of deploying her strategy from behind her desk, Caroline scooped up a small stack of manila folders atop it, invited Peyton and Ava to seat themselves on an overstuffed sofa on the opposite wall, then sat down in a matching chair beside it.

"May I call you Peyton?" she asked with a warm smile.

"Sure," he told her.

He waited for her to smile warmly at Ava and ask if she could call her by her first name, too, but Caroline instead began to sift through the folders until she homed in on one in particular.

Still smiling her warm smile—which Peyton would have sworn was genuine until she dismissed Ava so readily—she said, "I inputted your vital statistics, your likes and dislikes, and what you're looking for in a match into the computer, and I found four women I think you'll like very much. This one in particular," she added as she opened the top folder, "is quite a catch. Very old-money Chicago, born and raised here, Art Institute graduate, active volunteer in the local arts community, a curator for a small gallery on State Street, contributing reviewer for the *Tribune,* member of the Daughters of the American Revolution.... Oh, the list just goes on and on. She has every quality you're looking for."

Caroline handed the open folder to Peyton, who took it automatically. It contained a few sheets of printed information with a four-by-six head shot attached. It was to the latter that his gaze was naturally drawn. The woman was—well, there was no other word for it—breathtakingly beautiful. Okay, okay, that was two words, but that just went to show how amazingly gorgeous and incredibly dazzling she was. Women who looked like her just demanded adverbs to go along with the adjectives. Her hair was dark auburn and pooled around her bare shoulders; her eyes were huge, green and thickly lashed. He didn't kid himself that the photo wasn't retouched or that she would look the same had she not been so artfully made up with the kind of cosmetic wizardry that made a woman look as though she wasn't wearing makeup at all. She was still… Wow. Breathtakingly beautiful, amazingly gorgeous and incredibly dazzling.

"Wow," he said, speaking his thoughts aloud. Well, part of them, anyway. There were some that were best left in his head.

"Indeed," said Caroline with a satisfied smile. "Her name is—"

"Vicki," Ava finished, at the same time Caroline was saying, "Victoria."

The women exchanged looks, then spoke as one again. But, again, they each said something different.

"Victoria Haverty," said the matchmaker.

"Vicki Nielsson," said Ava.

The two women continued to stare at each other, but it was Caroline alone who spoke this time. "Do you know Ms. Haverty?"

Ava nodded. "Oh, yes. We debuted together. But Haverty is her maiden name. She's Vicki Nielsson now."

Caroline's eyes fairly bugged out of her head. "She's *married?*"

"I'm afraid so," Ava told her. "And living in Reykjavik with her husband, Dagbjart, last I heard. Which was about two weeks ago."

"But she gave me an address here in Chicago," Caroline objected, as if that would negate everything Ava had said.

"On Astor Street?" Ava asked.

Caroline went to her desk and tapped a few keys on a laptop sitting atop it. It was then that

Peyton realized all the information on his pages was nonidentifying statistics such as age, education, occupation and interests. "Yes," the matchmaker said without looking up.

"That's her parents' place," Ava replied. "She does come home to visit fairly often."

The matchmaker looked at Ava incredulously. "But why would she apply with a Chicago matchmaker if she's happily married and living in…um, where is Reykjavik?"

"Iceland," Peyton and Ava said in unison.

The matchmaker looked even more confused. "Why would she apply with Attachments if she's married and living in Iceland?"

When Peyton looked at Ava, she seemed to be trying very hard not to grin. A smug grin, too, if he wasn't mistaken. He knew that because she wasn't doing a very good job fighting it.

"Well," she began smugly, "maybe Vicki's not as happily married as ol' Dagbjart would like to think. And ol' Dagbjart is, well, ol'," she added. "He was seventy-six when Vicki married him. He must be pushing ninety by now. The Havertys have always been known for marrying into families even wealthier than they are, but clearly Vicki underestimated that Scandinavian life expectancy. Did you know men in Iceland live longer than men in any other country?"

The matchmaker said nothing in response to that. Neither did Peyton, for that matter. What could he say? Other than, *Hey, Caroline, way to go on the background checks.*

The matchmaker finally seemed to remember she was with a client who was paying her a crapload of money to find him a mate—a mate who wasn't already married, by the way—and returned to the sofa to snatch the folder out of Peyton's hands and replace it with another. "An honest mistake," she said. "I'm sure you'll like this one even better."

He opened that folder to find another sheet of vital statistics affixed to another four-by-six glossy, this time of a woman who wasn't quite as breathtaking, amazing or incredible as the first, but who was still beautiful, gorgeous and dazzling. She, too, had auburn hair, a few shades lighter than the first, and eyes so clear a blue, they could have only been enhanced with Photoshop. Still, even without retouching, the woman was stunning.

"This young woman," Caroline said, "is the absolute cream of Chicago society. One of her ancestors helped found the Chicago Mercantile Exchange and her father is on the Chicago Board of Trade. Her mother's family are the Lauderdales, who own the Lauderdale department store chain, among other things. She herself has two college degrees, one in business and one in fashion design. Her name is..."

The matchmaker hesitated, glancing over at Ava.

As if taking the cue, Ava looked at Peyton and said, "Roxy Mittendorf. Roxanne," she corrected herself when Caroline looked as if she would take exception. "But she went by Roxy when we were kids."

Now Ava was the one to hesitate, as if she were weighing whether or not to say more. Finally, the weight fell, and she added, "At least until after that college spring break trip, when she came home with the clap. Then people started calling her Doxy. I'm not sure if that's because they thought she was, you know, a doxy, or because her doctor prescribed doxycycline to treat it." She brightened. "But I guess that's really neither here nor there, is it? I mean, it's not like she still has the clap. At least, I don't think that's one that flares up again, is it?"

She traded glances with both Peyton and Caroline, and when neither of them commented, she evidently felt it necessary to add, "Well, *I* never called her Doxy. I didn't even find out about the clap thing until after graduation."

Peyton closed the file folder and handed it back to Caroline without comment. Caroline fished for the third in her lap and exchanged it for the second one. When he opened this one he found—taa-daa!—another redheaded beauty, this one with eyes a lighter blue that might actually occur in nature. Interesting that the matchmaker was three for three with regard to red hair.

When he glanced back at Caroline, she seemed to sense his thoughts, because she said, "Well, you did indicate you had a preference for redheads. And also green eyes, but except for that first, all my other candidates for you have blue eyes. Still, not so very different, right?"

For some reason—Peyton couldn't imagine why—they both looked over at Ava. Ava with her dark red hair and green, green eyes.

"What?" she asked innocently.

"Nothing," Peyton said, grateful she hadn't made the connection.

Had he actually stated on his application that he had a preference for green-eyed redheads? He honestly couldn't remember. Then again, he'd been on the jet heading to Chicago at the time, surrounded by a ton of work he'd wanted to finish before his arrival. He'd only been half paying attention to how he was answering the questions. He thought about several of the women he had dated in the past and was surprised to realize that most of them had been redheads. Odd. He liked all women. He didn't care if their hair was blond, brown, red or purple, or what color eyes they had, or what their ethnic, educational or economic origins were. If they were smart, funny and beautiful, if they made him feel good when he was with them, that was all he cared about. So why had he dated so many redheads? Especially when redheads were such a minority?

Instead of looking where he wanted to look just then, he turned his attention to his third prospective date. Before Caroline had a chance to say a word, he held up the photo to show Ava. "Do you know her?"

Ava looked almost guilty. "I do, actually. But you know her, too. She went to Emerson with us. She was in my grade."

Peyton looked at the photo again. The woman was in no way familiar. Which was weird, because a girl that pretty he would have remembered. "Are you sure? I don't remember her at all."

"Well, you should," Ava said. "You two played hockey together for three years."

He shook his head. "That's not possible. There weren't any girls on the Emerson hockey team."

"No, there weren't."

Understanding dawned on him then. Dawned like a good, solid blow to the back of the head. He looked at the photo again, shortening the hair and blunting the features a bit. "Oh, my God," he finally said. "Is that Nick Boorman?"

"Nicolette," Ava corrected him. "She goes by Nicolette now."

Peyton closed the folder and handed it back to Caroline. "Not that there's anything wrong with that," he said. "But it would just be kind of, um…"

"Awkward," Ava whispered helpfully.

"Yeah."

Caroline took the folder from him and tucked it under the other two candidates that were a no-go. But she was looking at Ava when she did it. "Who *are* you?" she asked.

Ava shrugged. "I'm just Mr. Moss's *assistant*."

Caroline didn't look anywhere near convinced. She lifted the last of her folders defiantly. She spoke not to Peyton this time, but to Ava. "*This* candidate has only lived in Chicago for four years. She's originally from Miami. Do you have any friends or family in Miami, Ms. Brenner? Any connection to that city at all?"

Ava shook her head. "No, I don't."

Caroline opened the folder and showed the

photo to Ava before allowing Peyton to look at it. "Do you know this woman?"

Ava shook her head again. "I haven't had the pleasure of meeting her. Yet," she added, seemingly pointedly.

"Good," Caroline said. She turned to Peyton and finally allowed him to view the file. "This is Francesca Stratton. She started off as a software developer but is now the CEO of her own company. Her father is a neurosurgeon in Coral Gables, and her mother is a circuit court judge for the state of Florida. Their lineage in that state goes back six generations. *And* she's a distant cousin to King Juan Carlos of Spain."

Now Caroline looked at Ava, as if daring her to come up with something that might challenge the woman's pedigree. When Ava only smiled benignly, the matchmaker continued, "Peyton, I think you and she would be perfect for each other."

He tried not to think about how Caroline had considered the three candidates ahead of Francesca more perfect, and instead took the file to look over the rest of the woman's particulars.

He liked that she had built her own company, the way he had, and her knowledge of computers and software design could definitely come in handy with regard to his own work. She was outdoorsy—she cited a love of scuba diving, rock climbing and horseback riding. She preferred nonfiction over fiction, rock and roll over any other music, eating out over eating in. And she was a fan of both the Florida Panthers and Chicago Blackhawks. There wasn't a single thing in her vitals to dissuade him from agreeing with Caroline. She really did seem perfect for him.

So why wasn't he more excited about the prospect of meeting her?

A movement to his left caught his eye, and he found Ava trying to read the file from where she sat. Instead of making her work for it, he handed it to her.

"What do you think?" he asked as she turned to the final page.

"Ivy League–educated, accomplished pianist, member of the United States Dressage Federation, one of Chicago's One Hundred Women Making a Difference. What's not to love?"

Funny, but she didn't sound as though she loved Francesca.

"So on the Jackie Kennedy scale," he said, "where do you think she'd fall?"

Ava closed the file and returned it to the matchmaker. "Well, if Jackie Kennedy were a young woman today, I think she'd be a lot like Francesca Stratton."

"So…maybe eight?"

With what sounded like much resignation and little satisfaction, she said, "Ten."

That was exactly what Peyton wanted to hear. So why was he disappointed hearing it?

In spite of his reaction, he turned to Caroline and said, "Sounds like we have a winner. When can you set something up?"

The matchmaker looked both relieved and happy. "Let me contact Francesca to see what works for her, and I'll get back to you. What evenings work best for you?"

"Just about any evening is fi—" Peyton started to say. But the delicate clearing of a throat to his left him kept him from finishing.

He looked over at Ava, who was shaking her head.

"What?" he asked.

"You said you didn't think you were ready to meet any of your prospective dates just yet," she reminded him.

"No, you said that."

"And you agreed. We still have several lessons we need to go over."

He said nothing. He had agreed. And really, he didn't mind that much putting off the meeting. Odd, since he really did want to get out of Chicago and back to San Francisco. Maybe he hadn't felt as antsy over the past few days as he had when he'd first arrived, but he did need to get back to the West Coast soon. So he and Ava needed to wrap things up pronto.

"How long do you think we'll need to get me through them?" he asked. And for some really bizarro reason, he found himself hoping she would tell him it would be weeks and weeks and weeks.

Instead, she told him, "Another week, at least."

"So maybe by the weekend after this one?"

She looked as if she wanted to say, *No, it will be weeks and weeks and weeks.* Instead, she replied, “Um, sure. If we work hard, and if you follow the rules,” she added meaningfully, “then we can probably get you where you need to be by then.”

Following the rules. Not his favorite thing to do. Still, if it would get him a date with a modern-day Jackie Kennedy…

He turned to Caroline again. “How about next Friday or Saturday if she’s available?”

Caroline jotted the dates down on the top of the file folder. “I’m reasonably certain that one of those days will be fine. I’ll let you know which one after I’ve spoken to Francesca.”

Great, he thought without much enthusiasm. “Great!” he said with much enthusiasm.

He stood, with Ava quickly following suit, thanked Caroline for all her work, and they both started to make their way to the door. They halted, however, when the matchmaker called Ava’s name.

“Ms. Brenner,” she said tentatively, “you, ah… you wouldn’t happen to be looking for a job, would you? Something part-time that wouldn't interfere with your work as Peyton's assistant? You'd be an enormous asset to us here at Attachments, Inc."

Looking a little startled, Ava replied, "Um, no. But thank you."

Peyton told Caroline, "The reason Ava knew all those women is because she moves in the same social circles they do. Her family is loaded. She doesn't have to work." Unable to help himself, he added, "Never mind that she's bleeding me dry for being my *assistant* at the moment."

Caroline suddenly looked way more interested in Ava than she had when Ava was just a prospective part-timer. Funny, though, how Ava suddenly looked kind of panicky.

"I see," the matchmaker said. "Well then, maybe *I* could help *you.* Introduce you to a nice man who has the same set of values you have?"

In other words, Peyton translated, a nice man who had the same *value* that Ava had. *Cha-ching.* For some reason, he suddenly felt kind of panicky, too.

"What do you say, Ava?" the matchmaker

added. And it wasn't lost on Peyton that she had switched to the first-name basis she evidently only used with her clients, not to mention the almost genuinely warm smile. "Would you like to fill out an application while you're here?"

Ava smiled back, but somehow looked even more alarmed. "Thank you, Caroline, but I'm really not in the market right now."

Her response made Peyton wonder again if she was seriously involved with someone, and if that was why she wasn't currently in the market. During the week the two of them had spent together, she had never said anything that made him think there was a significant other in her life, and she seemed to have plenty of time on her hands if she was able to work with him every day. Call him crazy, but he didn't think a guy who had a woman like Ava waiting for him at home—hell, who had *Ava* waiting for him at home—would be too happy about her spending so much time with another guy. If Peyton had Ava waiting at home for him, he'd sure as hell never—

But he didn't have Ava waiting at home for

him, he reminded himself. And he didn't want her waiting at home for him. So what was the point of even thinking about it?

"Well, if you change your mind..." Caroline said, leaving the statement incomplete but her intention stated.

"You'll be the first person I call," Ava promised.

Peyton did his best not to wish he could be the first person she'd call. Even though he kind of did.

Dammit, what was wrong with him? He'd just been paired up with a modern-day Jackie Kennedy. He should be over the moon. He was just distracted, that was all—too much going on. The takeover of Montgomery and Sons, massive self-improvement, the hunt for the right woman, the ghost of high school past...it was no wonder his brain was scrambled.

"Are we finished here?" he asked, more irritably than he intended.

Both Caroline and Ava seemed to notice that, too. But it was Ava who replied, "You tell me."

"Yes," he snapped.

Without awaiting a reply, he made his way to the door. Let the women draw whatever conclusion they wanted from his behavior. As far as he was concerned, any lessons Ava might have in store for the rest of the day were canceled. He had work to do. Work that didn't include anything or anyone with more than one X chromosome.

Six

Ava and Peyton sat on a bench at the Chicago Institute of Art studying Edward Hopper's *Nighthawks,* neither saying a word. She had instructed him to spend five minutes in silence taking in the details of several paintings that morning, but none of them had captured his attention the way this one had. It almost seemed as if he wanted to walk right into the painting and join the people sitting at the café bar for a cup of late-night coffee.

As he studied the painting, Ava studied him. He was wearing a different pair of dark-wash jeans today, with another fitted sweater—this one the color of good cognac that set off his amber eyes beautifully. She'd opted for a pair of tobacco-colored trousers and a dark green tailored shirt. She couldn't help thinking that, fashionwise, they complemented each other perfectly. But that was about the only compatibility the two of them were enjoying today.

He'd barely spoken to her after they left the matchmaker's office yesterday, barring one angry outburst that had left her flummoxed. After saying they were finished for the day, he'd offered to have his driver drop her at her house on the way back to his hotel, wherever her house was, since she hadn't told him her address, and why was that, anyway, did she still think he wasn't fit to enter the premises the way she had when they were kids, since he'd had to climb out the window when he left her house that one time he was there, not use the front door like a normal—meaning blue-blooded, filthy-rich—person would?

Ava had been stunned to momentary silence. Until then, they'd seemed to have an unspoken agreement that they would never, under any circumstances, specifically mention that night. Then she'd gathered herself enough to snap back that he could have used the front door if he'd wanted to, but he'd chosen to go out the window because he'd been too ashamed to be seen with her, reeking of old money as she was, which was at least better than reeking of gasoline and gutter scum.

What followed might have been an explosion of resentment and frustration that had been steeping for sixteen years. Instead, both had been too horrified by what they'd said to each other, by what they knew they could never take back, that neither had said another word. Neither had apologized, either. They'd just looked out their respective windows until they reached Talk of the Town. Ava had hopped out of the car with a hastily uttered instruction for Peyton to meet her at the Art Institute this morning and slammed the door before he could object.

Neither had mentioned the exchange today. Their conversation had focused exclusively on art commentary, but it had been civil. In spite of that, a stagnant uneasiness surrounded them, and neither seemed to know what to do to ease it.

She glanced at her watch and saw that the five minutes she'd asked Peyton to give to the painting had become eight. Instead of telling him time was up, she turned her attention to the painting, too. It was one she had responded to immediately the first time she'd seen it, during an Emerson Academy field trip when she was in ninth grade. The people in the painting had always looked to her as if they were displaced and at loose ends, as though they were just biding their time in the diner while they waited for something—anything—to change.

The painting still spoke to her that way. Except that now the people looked lonely, too.

"I like how the light is brightest on the guy behind the counter," Peyton said suddenly, stirring Ava from her thoughts. "It makes him look like some kind of…I don't know…spiritual figure or something. He's the guy providing the sustenance, but maybe that sustenance is more than coffee and pie, you know?"

Ava turned to look at him, surprised at the pithiness of the comment.

Before she could say anything, and still looking at the picture, he added, “What’s also interesting is that the only real color on the people is with the woman, and both times, it’s warm colors. The red on her dress, and the orange in her hair. Although maybe I only notice that because I’ve always been partial to redheads.”

He’d said the same thing at the matchmaker’s, she recalled. Or, at least, Caroline had said that was what he’d stated on his questionnaire. Just as he had yesterday after the comment, he turned to look at Ava…then at Ava’s hair. Warmth oozed through her belly, because he looked at her now the way he had that night at her parents’ house. The two of them had been sitting on the floor in her bedroom, bleary-eyed from their studies, when Ava had cupped the back of her neck, complaining of an incessant ache. Peyton had uncharacteristically taken pity on her and moved her hand to place his there, rubbing gently to ease the knot. One minute, the two of them had been overtaxed and stressed by their homework, and the next…

"I mean…" he sputtered. "That is…it's just…uh…"

"That's so interesting, what you said about the light and the guy behind the counter," she interrupted, pretending she didn't understand why he suddenly seemed edgy. Pretending she didn't feel edgy herself. "I've never thought about that before."

Instead of turning his attention back to the painting, Peyton continued to look at Ava. Oh, God, that was all she needed. If they followed the pattern from sixteen years ago, the two of them were going to end up horizontal on the bench, fully entwined and half-naked. That was how it had been that night at her parents' house. The first time, anyway—they'd been on each other so fast, so fiercely, that they'd only managed to undo any buttons and zippers that were in their way. The second time had been much more leisurely, much more thorough. Where the first time had been a physical act intended to release pressure, the second time had been much more…

"In fact," Ava hurried on, looking back at the painting herself, "it's the sort of interpretation that might lead to a discussion that could go on for hours."

Her heart was racing, and heat was seeping into her chest and face. So she made herself do what she'd done in high school whenever she started reacting that way to Peyton. She channeled her inner Gold Coast ice princess—who she was dismayed to find still lurked beneath the surface—and forced herself to be distant, methodical…and not a little bitchy. She was Peyton's teacher, not his…not someone who should be experiencing odd, decades-old feelings she never should have felt in the first place. She'd never be able to compete with a modern-day Jackie Kennedy anyway. She was the last sort of woman Peyton wanted or needed to accomplish his goals.

"Which is exactly why," she said frostily, "I don't want you saying things like that."

Sensing his annoyance at her crisp tone, she

pressed on. She didn't dwell on how she was behaving exactly the way she had sworn not to—treating him the way she had in high school—but she was starting to feel way too many things she shouldn't be feeling, and she didn't know what else to do.

"What I really want for you to take away from this exercise," she told him coolly, "is something less insightful. That shouldn't be too difficult, should it?"

"*Less* insightful?" he echoed. "I thought the whole point of this museum thing was to teach me how to say something about art that wouldn't make me sound like an idiot."

She nodded. "Which is why I've focused on the works I have today. These are artists and paintings that are familiar to everyone. For your purposes, you only need to master some passing art commentary. Not deep, pithy insight."

"Then tell me, oh great art guru," he said sarcastically, "what do I need to know about this one?"

Looking at the painting, again—since it was better than looking at the angry expression on

Peyton's face—Ava said, "You should say how interesting it is that the themes in *Nighthawks* are similar to Hopper's *Sunlight in a Cafeteria,* but that the perspective of time is reversed."

"But I haven't seen *Sunlight in a Cafeteria,*" he pointed out. "Not to mention I don't know what the fu— Uh…what you're talking about."

"No one else you'll be talking to has seen it, either," she assured him. "And you don't have to understand it. The minute you offer some indication that you know more about art than your companion, they'll change the subject." She smiled her cool, disaffected smile and told him, "I think you're good to go with the major players in American art. Tomorrow, we'll take on the Impressionists. Then, if we have time, the Dutch masters."

Peyton groaned. "Oh, come on, Ava. How often is this stuff really going to come up in conversation?"

"More often than you think. And we still have to cover books and music, too."

He eyed her flatly. "There's no way I need to know all this stuff before my date with Francesca. I don't need to know it for moving in business circles, either. I think you're just stalling."

Ava gaped at him. "That's ridiculous. Why would I want to spend more time with you than I have to?"

"Got me," he shot back. "God knows it's not like you need the money I'm sure you'll charge me for overtime. I think I've got all this…stuff…covered. Let's move on."

Well, at least he was abiding by the no-profanity rule, she thought. She decided not to comment on the other part of his charge. "Music," she reiterated instead. "Books."

He expelled an exasperated breath. "Fine. I've been a huge Charles Dickens fan since high school. How's that?"

She couldn't quite hide her surprise. "You read Charles Dickens for fun?"

He clamped his jaw tight. "Yeah." More icily, he added, "And Camus and Hemingway, too. Guess that comes as a shock to you, doesn't it? That gasoline-reeking gutter scum like me could have understood anything other than the sports stats in the *Sun-Times*."

"Peyton, that wasn't what I was think—"

"The hell it wasn't."

So much for the profanity rule. Not that Ava called him on it, since she was kind of responsible for its being broken. She started to deny her charge, then stopped. "Okay, maybe that was kind of what I was thinking. But you didn't exactly show your brainy side in school. Still, I'm sorry. I shouldn't have assumed that. Especially in light of what you've accomplished since then."

He seemed surprised—and a little confused—by her apology. He didn't let her off the hook, though. "And in light of what I accomplished then, too," he added. "Which was something you never bothered to discover for yourself."

Now it was Ava's turn to be surprised. He still sounded hurt by something that had happened—or, rather, hadn't happened—half a lifetime ago. Nevertheless, she told him, "I wasn't the only one who didn't bother to get to know my classmates. I was more than I appeared to be in high school, too, Peyton, but did you ever notice or care?"

He uttered an incredulous sound. "Right. More

than just a beautiful shell filled with nothing but self-interest? I don't think so."

"You don't *think* so?" she echoed. "Present tense? You still think I'm just a—" She halted herself, thinking it would be best to skirt the whole *beautiful* thing. "I'm just a shell filled with nothing but self-interest?"

He said nothing, only continued to look at her the way the teenage Peyton had.

"You think the reason I'm helping you out like this is all for *myself?*" she asked. "You don't think maybe I'm doing it because it's a nice thing for me to do for an old…for a former classmate?"

Now he barked in disbelief. "You're doing it because I'm paying you a bucket of money. If that isn't self-interest, I don't know what is."

There was no way she could set him straight without revealing the reality of her situation. Of course, she *could* do that. She could tell him about how she had walked in his figurative shoes her senior year. She could tell him how she understood now the battles between pride and shame, and desire and need, and how each day had been filled with wondering how she was going to survive into the next one. She could tell him how she'd listened to her mother crying in the next room every night, and how she had forbidden herself to do the same, because nothing could come from that. She could tell him how she'd stood in the yard of the Milhouse Prewitt School every morning and steeled herself before going in, only to be worn to a nub by day's end by the relentless bullying.

Just do it, Ava. Be honest with him. Maybe then karma really will smile upon you.

But on the heels of that thought came another: *Or maybe Peyton will laugh and say the same things you heard every day at Prewitt, about looking like you live in a box under a bridge, and stealing extra fruit from the lunch line—don't think we haven't seen you do it, Ava—and not being fit to clean the houses of your classmates because no one wants their house smelling the way you smell, and maybe you don't live in box under a bridge, after all, maybe you live in a Dumpster.*

She opened her mouth, honestly not sure what would come out. And she heard herself say,

"Right. I forgot. Money and social standing are more important to me than anything." Conjuring her before-the-fall high school self again, she cocked her head to one side and smiled an icy smile. In a voice that could freeze fire, she said, "But that's because they *are* more important than anything, aren't they, Peyton? That's something you've learned, too, isn't it? That's what you want more than anything now. Guess that makes us two of a kind."

His mouth dropped open, as if it had never occurred to him how much he resembled the people for whom he'd had so much contempt in high school. The two of them really had switched places. In more than just a social context. In a philosophical one, as well. She understood better than ever now that what defined a person was their character, not what kind of car was parked in their garage or what kind of clothes hung in their closet. She was poor in an economic sense, but she was rich in other ways—certainly richer than the integrity-starved girl she'd been in high school.

Peyton, on the other hand, had money to burn,

but was running short on integrity, if what he'd told her about his business methods were any indication. He'd thrust plenty of families into the sort of life he'd clawed his way out of. And he was currently trying to take a family business away from the last remaining members of that family, to plunder and dismember it. He'd be putting even more people out of work and more families on the dole. And he was going to do it under the manufactured guise of being a decent, mannerly individual. Really, which one of them had the most to feel guilty about these days?

"I think we've both had enough for today," she said decisively.

"We finally get to escape the museum?" he asked with feigned hopefulness, still looking plenty irritated by her last remark.

"Yes, we've had enough of that, too. Since it looks like you have the literary angle covered, tomorrow we can tackle music."

He looked as if he were going to protest, then the fight seemed to go out of him. "Okay. Fine. Whatever. What time should I pick you up?"

She shook her head, as she did every time he asked that question—and he'd asked it every day. She said the same thing she always said in response. "I'll meet you."

Before he could object—something else he did every day—she gave him the address of a jazz record store on East Illinois and told him to be there when they opened.

"And then I bet we get to have lunch at another pretentious restaurant," he said, sounding as weary as she felt. "Hey, I know. I'll even wear one of my new suits this time."

She knew he meant for the comment to be sarcastic. So she only echoed his ennui back. "Okay. Fine. Whatever."

Ennui. Right. As if the tension and fatigue they were feeling could be ascribed to a lack of interest. Then again, maybe for Peyton, it was. He'd made no secret about his reluctance to be My Fair Gentlemanned to within an inch of his life. He really didn't give a damn about any of this and was only doing it to further his business. Ava wished she could share his disinterest.

The reason for her impatience and irritation this week had nothing to do with not caring.

And it had everything to do with caring too much.

Seven

Peyton gazed at Ava from across the smallest table he'd ever been forced to sit at and did his best to ignore the ruffled lavender tablecloth and flowered china tea set atop it. He tried even harder to ignore the cascade of lace curtains to his right and the elaborately scrolled ironwork tea caddy to his left. And it would be best not to get him started on the little triangular sandwiches with the crusts cut off or the mountain of frothy pastries.

Tea. She was actually making him *take tea* with her. In a tea shop. Full of women in hats and gloves. Hell, even Ava was wearing a hat and gloves. A little white hat with one of those netted veil things that fell over her eyes, and white gloves that went halfway up her arm with a bazillion buttons. Her white dress had even more buttons than her gloves did.

She hadn't been wearing the hat or gloves when she'd walked into the record store earlier, so he hadn't realized what was in store for him. She'd pulled them out of her oversize purse as the two of them rode to the damned *tea* shop—except she hadn't said they were going to a *tea* shop. She'd said they were going to a late lunch.

Still, the appearance of a hat and gloves should have been his first clue that "lunch" was going to be even worse than something he'd put on a damned suit for. Something that would, in Ava's words, aid in his edification. He just wished he could believe this was for his edification instead of being some kind of punishment for his behavior at the museum yesterday.

He also wished he could think Ava looked ridiculous in her dainty alabaster frock and habiliments. Which was the kind of language to use for a getup like that, even if those were words he had always—before this week, anyway—manfully avoided. Hell, she looked as if she was an escapee from an overbudgeted period film set during the First World War. Unfortunately, there was something about the getup that was also... Well... Dammit. Unbelievably hot.

Which was just what he needed. To be turned on by Ava, the last woman on the planet who should be turning him on. He'd been so sure he could remain unaffected by her while they were undertaking this self-improvement thing. After all, they hadn't gotten along at all that first morning at her apartment. Instead, with every passing day, he'd just become more bewitched by her.

Just as he had in high school.

It was only physical, he told himself. The same way it had only been physical in high school. There was just some kind of weird chemistry between them. Her pheromones talking to his pheromones or something. Talking, hell. More like screaming at the top of their lungs. People didn't have to like each other to be sexually attracted to each other. They just had to have loud, obnoxious pheromones.

Tea, he reminded himself distastefully. *Focus on the fact that she's making you sit in a tea-room drinking—gak—*tea *and eating the kind of stuff that no self-respecting possessor of a Y chromosome should ingest.* God knew what this was going to do to his testosterone levels.

"Now then," she said in a voice that was every bit as prissy as her outfit. "Taking tea. This will probably be your biggest challenge yet."

Oh, Peyton didn't doubt that for a minute. What he did doubt was that many people actually *took tea*—he just couldn't think that phrase in anything but a snotty tone of voice…tone of mind…whatever—in this country. Not any people with a Y chromosome, anyway.

"A lot of people think the art of tea has fallen by the wayside over the years," she continued, obviously reading his mind. Or maybe his distasteful expression. "But it's actually been rising in popularity. Hence your need to be familiar with it."

"Ava," he said, mustering as much patience as

he could, "I think I can safely say that no matter how high in society I go, I will never, ever, ask anyone to—" he could barely get the words out of his mouth "—*take tea* with me."

She smiled a benign smile. "I bet the sisters Montgomery would be charmed by a man who asked them to tea. And I bet not one of your competitors would think to do it."

She was right. Dammit. Two sweet old Southern ladies would find this place enchanting. Crap. *Enchanting.* There was another word he normally avoided manfully. Where the hell had his testosterone gotten off to?

He blew out an exasperated breath. "Fine. Just don't expect me to wear white gloves."

"I suppose we could allow that small concession," she agreed. "Now then. As Henry James wrote in *The Portrait of a Lady,* 'There are few hours in life more agreeable than the hour dedicated to the ceremony known as afternoon tea.'"

Oh, good. At least this wouldn't last more than an hour.

"And I, for one," she continued, "couldn't agree more."

Peyton did his best to look as if he gave a crap. "Yeah, well, ol' Henry obviously never spent an afternoon sharing a case of Anchor Steam with his friends while the Blackhawks trounced the Canucks."

Ava smiled thinly. "No doubt."

She launched into a monologue about the history of afternoon tea—all three centuries of it—then moved on to the etiquette of afternoon tea, then on to the menu selection of afternoon tea. She talked about the differences between cream tea, light tea and full tea—thankfully, they were having full tea, since Peyton was getting hungrier with every word she spoke—then she pointed to the selections on the caddy beside them, categorizing them as savories, scones and pastries, even though they looked to him like sandwiches, biscuits and dessert. By the time she wrapped up her dissertation, his stomach was grumbling so forcefully even his Y chromosome was thinking the little flowery cakes looked good.

Unfortunately, as he reached for one, Ava smacked his hand as if he were a toddler.

"Don't reach," she said. "Ask for them to be passed."

"But they're sitting right there."

"They're closer to me than they are to you."

"Oh, sure, by an inch and a half."

"Nonetheless, whoever is closer should pass to the person who is farther away."

Okay, she was definitely going out of her way to be ornery, deliberately to get a rise out of him. Well, he'd show her. He'd kill her with kindness. He'd be as courteous as he knew how to be. And thanks to her lessons, he'd learned how to be pretty damned courteous.

Sitting up straighter in his tiny chair, he channeled the inner Victorian he didn't even know he possessed and said, "If you please, Miss Brenner, and if it wouldn't trouble you overly, would you pass the…" What had she called them? "The savories?"

She eyed him suspiciously, clearly doubting his sincerity. But what was she going to do? He'd been a perfect effing gentleman. He'd even thought the word *effing,* instead of what he really wanted to think, which was…uh, never mind.

Still looking at him as if she expected him to start a food fight, she asked, "May I suggest the cucumber sandwiches or the crab puffs?"

He unclenched his jaw long enough to reply, "You may."

"Which would you prefer?"

"The cucumber sandwiches," he said. Mostly because he didn't think he could say *crab puffs* with a straight face. Not that *cucumber sandwiches* was exactly easy. "If you please."

Before retrieving the plate, she began to unbutton her gloves. Evidently good manners precluded wearing such garments whilst one was taking tea.

Dammit, he thought when he played that back in his head. There was no way he was going to last an hour in this place.

When she finally had her gloves off—a good fortnight after initiating their unbuttoning—she reached for the plate of sandwiches and passed it the three inches necessary to place it on the table between them. Then she poured them each a cup of tea from the pot, adding three sugar cubes—jeez, they had flowers on them, too—

to her own. Peyton eschewed them—since no one taking tea would ever *blow off* something; they would always *eschew* it—and lifted the cup to his mouth. At Ava's discreetly cleared throat, he looked up, and she tilted her head toward the cup he was holding. Holding by its bowl having grabbed the entire thing in his big paw, because he'd been afraid he'd break off the handle if he tried to pick it up that way. Gah. After a moment of juggling, he managed the proper manipulation of the cup, holding it by its handle, if just barely. Only then did Ava nod her head to let him know he was allowed to continue.

Man, had she actually had to grow up this way? Had her mother sat her down, day after day, and made her memorize all the stuff she was making him memorize? Had she been forced to dress a certain way and unfold her napkin just so, and talk about only approved subjects with other people, the way she was teaching him to do? Or did that just come naturally to people who were born with the bluest blood in the highest income bracket? Was good taste and polite behavior encoded on her DNA the way green eyes and red hair were? Did refinement run in her veins? And if so, did that mean Peyton's DNA was encoded with garbage-strewn streets and fighting dirty and that transmission fluid flowed through his veins?

It hit him again, even harder, how far apart the two of them were. How far apart they'd been since birth. How far apart they'd be until they died. Even with his income rivaling hers now, even mastering all these lessons that would grant him access to her world, he'd never, ever be her social equal. Because he'd never, ever be as comfortable with this stuff as she was. It would never be second nature to him the way it was to her. He would hate it in her world. All the rules and customs would suffocate him. It would kill everything that made him who he was, the same way taking Ava *out* of her world would doubtless suffocate her and kill everything that made her her.

And why did it bug him so much to realize that? He wasn't a kid anymore. He didn't care what world she lived in or that he'd never be granted citizenship there. Truth be told, now that he was a monster success, he kind of reveled in his mean-streets background. Even as a teenager, he'd taken a perverse sort of pride in where he came from, because where he came from hadn't destroyed his spirit the way it had so many others in the neighborhood. So why had it been such a sticking point with him in high school, the vast socioeconomic chasm between him and Ava? Why was it still a sticking point now, when that chasm had shrunk to a crack? Why did it bother him so much that his and Ava's worlds would never meet? What difference did her presence in the scheme of things—or lack thereof—make anyway?

His cup was nearly to his mouth when an answer to that question exploded in his head. It bothered him, he suddenly knew, because the thing that had sparked his success, the thing that had made him escape his neighborhood and muscle his way into a top-tier college, the thing that had kept him from giving up the hundreds of times he wanted to give up, the thing that had made him seize the business world with both fists and driven him to make money, and then more money, and then more money still…the thing that had done all that was…

Hell. It wasn't a thing at all. It was a person. It was Ava.

Down went the teacup, landing on the table with a thump that sent some of its contents spilling onto his hand. Peyton scarcely felt the burn. He looked at Ava, who was studying a plate of cakes and cookies, trying to decide which one she wanted. She was oblivious to both his spilled tea and tumultuous thoughts, but she had flipped back the veil from her face, leaving her features in clear profile.

She really hadn't changed since high school. Not just her looks, but the rest of her, too. She was as beautiful now as she'd been then, as elegant, as refined. And, he couldn't help thinking further, as off-limits. When all was said and done, the Ava of adulthood was no different from the Ava of adolescence. And neither was he. He was still—and would always be—the basest kind of interloper in her world.

As if to hammer home their differences, she finally decided on a frilly little pastry cup filled with berries and whipped cream and transferred it to her plate with a pair of dainty little silver tongs. Then she went for one of the prissy little flowered cakes. Then a couple of the lacy little cookies. All the fragile little things Peyton would have been afraid of touching because he would probably crush them. He was way better suited to a big, bloody hunk of beef beside a mountain of stiff mashed potatoes, with a sweaty longneck bottle of beer to wash it all down. The nectar of the working-class male.

When Ava finally looked up to see how he was faring, her brows knitted downward in confusion. He glanced at the plate of sandwiches sitting between them. Although they were heartier than the pastries, those, too, looked just as off-limits as everything else, so small and delicate and pretty were they. He tried to focus on them anyway, pretending to be indecisive about which one he wanted. But his thoughts were still wrapped up in his epiphany. *God. Ava.* It had been Ava all along.

He wasn't trying to master the art of fine living because he wanted to take over another company and add another zero to his bottom line. Not really. Sure, taking over Montgomery and Sons was the impetus, but he wouldn't be trying to do that if it weren't for Ava. He wouldn't have done anything over the past sixteen years if it weren't for Ava. He'd still be in the old neighborhood, working in the garage with his old man. He'd be spending his days under the chassis of a car, then going home at night to an apartment a few blocks away to watch the Hawks, Bulls or Cubs while consuming a carryout value meal and popping open a cold one.

And, hell, he might have even been happy doing that. Provided he'd never met Ava.

But from the moment he'd laid eyes on her in high school, something had pushed him to rise above his lot in life. Not even pushed him. *Driven* him. Yeah, that was a better word. Because after Ava had walked into his life, nothing else had mattered. Nothing except bringing himself up to standards she might approve of. So that maybe, someday, she *would* approve of him. And so that maybe, someday, the two of them…

He didn't allow himself to finish the thought.

He was afraid of what else he might discover about himself. Bad enough he understood what had brought him this far. But he did understand now. Too well. What he didn't understand was why. Why had Ava had that effect on him when nothing else had? Why would he have been satisfied with the blue-collar life for which he had always assumed he was destined until he met her? What was it about her that had taken up residence deep inside him? Why had she been the catalyst for him to escape the mean streets when the mean streets themselves hadn't been enough to do that?

"Is something wrong?" she asked, pulling him out of his musings.

"No," he answered quickly. "Just trying to decide what I want."

Which was true, he realized. He just didn't want anything that was on the plate of sandwiches.

"The petit fours here are delicious," she told him.

He'd just bet they were. If he knew what the hell a petit four was.

"Though you'd probably prefer something a little more substantial."

Oh, no doubt.

"Maybe one of the curried-egg sandwiches? They're not the kind of thing you get every day."

And naturally Peyton didn't want the kind of thing he could get every day. Hell, that was the whole problem.

"Or if you want something sweeter…"

He definitely wanted something sweeter.

"…you might try one of the ginger cakes."

Except not that.

Oh, man, this thing with Ava wasn't turning out the way he'd planned *at all.* She was supposed to be schooling him in the basics of social climbing, not advanced soul-searching. And what man wanted to discover the workings of his inner psyche for the first time in a frickin' tearoom?

"Aaahhh…" he began, stringing the word over several time zones in an effort to stall. Finally, he finished, "Yeah. Gimme one of those curried-egg sandwiches. They sound absolutely…" The word was out of his mouth before he could stop it, so overcome by his surroundings, and so weakened by his musings, had he become. "Scrumptious."

Okay, that did it. With that terrible word, he could feel what little was left of his testosterone oozing out of every pore. A man could only take so much tea and remain, well, manly. And a man could only take so much self-discovery and remain sane. If Peyton didn't get out of this place soon…if he didn't get away from Ava soon…if he didn't get someplace, anyplace, far away from here—far away from *her*—ASAP, someplace where he could look inside himself and figure out what the hell was going on in his brain…

Bottom line, he just had to get outta here. Now.

"Look, Ava, do you mind if we cut this short?" he asked. "I just remembered a conference call I'm supposed to be in on in—" He looked at his watch and pretended to be shocked at the time. "Wow. Thirty minutes. I really need to get back to my hotel."

She looked genuinely crushed. "But the tea…"

"Can we get a doggie bag?"

Judging by the way her expression changed,

he might as well have just asked her if he could jump up onto the table, whip off his pants and introduce everyone to Mr. Happy.

"No," she said through gritted teeth. "One does not ask for a doggie bag for one's afternoon tea. Especially not in a place like this."

"Well, I don't know why the hell not," he snapped.

Oh, yeah. There it was. With even that mild profanity, he sucked some of his retreating testosterone back in. Now if he could just figure out how to reclaim the rest of it…

He glanced around until he saw a waiter—or whatever passed for a waiter in this place, since they were all dressed like maître d's—and waved the guy down in the most obnoxious way he knew how.

"Hey, you! Garson!" he shouted, deliberately mispronouncing the French word for *waiter.* "Could we get a doggie bag over here?"

Everyone in the room turned to stare at him—and Ava—in frank horror. That, Peyton had to admit, helped a lot with his masculine recovery. Okay, so he was acting like a jerk, and doing it at

Ava's expense. Sometimes, in case of emergency, a man had to break the glass on his incivility. No, on his crudeness, he corrected himself. His grossness. His bad effin' manners. Those were way better words for what he was tapping into. And wow, did it feel good.

He braved a glance at Ava and saw that she had propped her elbows on the table and dropped her head into her hands.

"Yo, Ava," he said. "Take your elbows off the table. That is so impolite. Everyone is staring at us. Jeez, I can't take you anywhere." He looked back at the waiter, who hadn't budged from the spot where he had been about to serve a couple of elderly matrons from a pile of flowered cakes. "What, am I not speakin' English here?" he yelled. Funny, but he seemed to have suddenly developed a Bronx accent. "Yeah, you in the penguin suit. Could we get a doggie bag for our—" he gestured toward the tea caddy and the plates on the table "—for all this stuff? I mean, at these prices, I don't want it to go to waste. Know what I'm sayin'?"

"Peyton, what are you doing?" Ava asked

from behind her hands. "Are you trying to get us thrown out of here?"

Wasn't that obvious? Was he really not speakin' English here?

"Garson!" he shouted again. "Hey, we don't got all day."

Ava groaned softly from behind her hands, then said something about how she would never be able to take tea here again. It was all Peyton could do not to reply, *You're welcome.*

Instead, he continued to channel his inner bad-mannered adolescent—who he wasn't all that surprised to discover lurked just beneath his surface. "The service in this place sucks, Ava. Next time, we should hit Five Guys instead. At least they give you your food in a bag. I don't think this guy's going to bring us one."

He figured he'd said enough now to make her snap up her head and blast him for being such a jerk—as politely as she could, naturally, since they were in a public place. Instead, when she dropped her hands, she just looked tired. Really, really tired. And she didn't say a word. She only stood, gathered her purse and gloves, turned her back, and walked away with all the elegance of a czarina.

Peyton was stunned. She wasn't going to say something combative in response? She wasn't going to call him uncouth? She wasn't going to tell him how it was men like him who gave his entire gender a bad name? She wasn't going to glare daggers or spit fire? She was just going to walk away without even trying?

When he realized that yep, that was exactly what she was going to do, he bolted after her. He was nearly to the exit when he realized they hadn't paid their bill, so ran back to the table long enough to drop a handful of twenties on top of it. He didn't wait for change. Hell, their server deserved a 100-percent tip for the way he had just behaved.

When he vaulted out of the tearoom onto the street, he found himself drowning in a river of people making the Friday-afternoon jump start from work to weekend. He looked left, then right, but had no idea which way Ava had gone. Remembering her outfit, he searched for a splash of white amid the sullen colors of business suits, driving his gaze in every direction. Finally, he spotted her, in the middle of a crosswalk at the end of the block, buttoning up those damned white gloves, as if she were Queen Elizabeth on her way to address the royal guard.

He hurtled after her, but by the time he made it to the curb, she was on the other side of the street and the light was changing. Not that that deterred him. As he sprinted into the crosswalk against the light, half a dozen drivers honked their displeasure, and he was nearly clipped by more than one bumper. Even when he made it safely to the other side of the street, he kept running, trying to catch up to the wisp of white that was Ava.

Every time he thought he was within arm's reach, someone or something blocked him from touching her, and for every step he took forward, she seemed to take two. Panic welled in him that he would never reach her, until she turned a corner onto a side street that was much less crowded. Still, he had to lengthen his stride to catch up with her, and still, for a moment, it seemed he never would. Finally, he drew near enough to grasp her upper arm and spin her around to face him. She immediately jerked out of his hold, swinging her handbag as she came. Peyton let her go, dodging her bag easily, then lifted both hands in surrender.

"Ava, I'm sorry," he said breathlessly. "But... Stop. Just stop a minute. Please."

For a moment, they stood there on the sidewalk looking at each other, each out of breath, each poised for...something. Peyton had no idea what. Ava should have looked ridiculous in her turn-of-the-century garb, brandishing her handbag in her little white gloves, her netted hat dipping to one side. Instead, she seemed ferocious enough to snap him in two. A passerby jostled him from behind, sending him forward a step, until he was nearly toe to toe with her. She took a step in retreat, never altering her pose.

"Leave me alone," she said without preamble.

"No," he replied just as succinctly.

"Leave me alone, Peyton," she repeated adamantly. "I'm going home."

"No."

He wasn't sure whether he uttered the word in

response to her first sentence or the second, but really, it didn't matter. He wasn't going to leave her alone, and he didn't want her to go home. Despite his conviction only moments ago that he needed to be by himself to sort out his thoughts, isolation was suddenly the last thing he wanted. Not that he was sure what the *first* thing was that he wanted, but… Well, okay, maybe he did kind of know what the first thing was that he wanted. He just wasn't sure he knew what to do with it if he got it. Well, okay, maybe he did kind of know that, too, but…

"You said we still have a lot of work to do before I can go out with Francesca," he reminded her, shoving his thoughts to the back of his brain and hoping they stayed there. "That's only a week away."

She relaxed her stance, dropping her purse to her side. It struck him again that she looked tired. He couldn't remember ever seeing her looking like that before. Not since reacquainting himself with her in Chicago. Not when they were kids. It was…unsettling.

Then he remembered that yes, he had seen her

that tired once. That night at her parents' house when they'd been up so late studying. It had unsettled him then, too. Enough that he'd wanted to do something to make her less weary. Enough that he'd placed his hands on her shoulders to rub away the knots in her tense muscles. But the moment he'd touched her—

He pushed that thought to the back of his brain, too. He *really* didn't need to be thinking about that right now.

"You should have thought about your date with Francesca before you humiliated us the tearoom," she said.

"Yeah, about that," he began. Not that he had any idea what to say about that, but *about that* seemed like a good start.

Ava spared him, however. "Peyton, we could work for a year, and it wouldn't make any difference. You'll just keep sabotaging us."

He couldn't help noting her use of the word *us*. She hadn't said he was sabotaging himself. She hadn't said he was sabotaging her efforts. She'd said he was sabotaging the two of them. He wondered if she noticed, too, how she'd lumped the two of them together, or if she even realized she'd said it. Even if she did, what did it mean, if anything?

"I only sabotaged us today," he told her. "And only because you were going out of your way to make things harder than they had to be."

Even though that was true, it wasn't why he'd behaved the way he had. He'd done that because he'd needed to get out of that place as fast as he could. The problem now was convincing Ava that he still wanted to move forward after deliberately taking so many giant steps backward.

And the problem was that, suddenly, his wanting to continue with this ridiculous makeover had less to do with winning over the Montgomery sisters in Mississippi…and more to do with winning over Ava right here in Chicago.

Eight

Ava trudged up the stairs to her apartment with Peyton two steps behind, silently willing him to twist his ankle. Not enough to do any permanent damage. Just enough to make him have to sit down and rub it for a few minutes so she could escape him.

In spite of her demands to leave her alone, he had followed her for three blocks, neither of them saying a word. She'd thought he would give up when they reached the door behind the shop that opened onto the stairwell leading up to her apartment. But he'd stuck his foot in it before she had a chance to slam it in his face. At this point, she was too tired to argue with him. If he wanted to follow her all the way up so she could slam her apartment door in his face, then that was his prerogative.

But he was too fast for her there, as well, shoving the toe of his new Gucci loafer between door and jamb before she had a chance to make the two connect. She leaned harder on the door, trying to put enough force into it that he would have to remove his foot or risk having his toes crushed. But his shoe held firm. Damn the excellence of Italian design anyway.

"Ava, let me in," he said, curling his fingers around the door and pushing back.

"Go. Away," she told him. Again.

"Just talk to me for a few minutes. Please?"

She sighed wearily and eased up on the door. Peyton shouldered it harder, gaining enough ground to win access to the apartment. But he halted halfway in, clearly surprised by his success. His face was scant inches from Ava's, and his fingertips on the door skimmed hers. Even though she was still wearing her white gloves, she could feel the warmth of his hand against hers. He was close enough for her to see how the amber of his irises was circled by a thin line of gold. Close enough for her to see a small scar on his chin that hadn't been there in high school. Close enough for her to smell the faint scent of something cool and spicy that clung to him. Close enough for her to feel his heat mingling with her own.

Close enough for her to wish he would move closer still.

Which was why she sprang away from the door and hurried toward the kitchen. Tea, she told herself. That was what she needed. A nice, calming cup of tea. She'd hardly had a chance to taste hers in the shop. She had a particularly soothing chamomile that would be perfect. Anything to take her thoughts off wanting to be close to Peyton. *No!* she quickly corrected herself. Anything to take her thoughts off her lousy afternoon.

Without wasting a moment to remove her gloves or hat—barely even taking the time to shove the netting of the latter back from her face—she snatched the kettle from the stove, filled it with water and returned it to the burner as she spun the knob to turn it on. Then she busied herself with retrieving the tea canister from the cupboard and searching a drawer for the strainer. She felt Peyton's gaze on her the entire time, so knew he had followed as far as the kitchen, but she pretended not to notice. Instead, after readying the tea and cup, she began sorting through other utensils in the drawer, trying to look as if she were searching for something else that was very important—like her peace of mind, since that had completely fled.

"Ava," he finally said when it became clear she wouldn't continue the conversation.

"What?" she asked, still focused on the contents of the drawer.

"Will you please talk to me?"

"Are we not talking?" she asked, not looking up. "It sounds to me as if we're talking. If we're not talking, then what are we doing?"

"I don't know what you're doing, but I'm trying to get you to look at me so I can explain why I did what I did earlier."

He wasn't going to leave until they'd hashed

this out. So she halted her phony search and slammed the drawer shut, turning to face him fully. "You were trying to get us thrown out of there on purpose," she said.

"You're right. I was," he admitted, surprising her.

He stood in the entry to the kitchen, filling it, making the tiny space feel microscopic. During their walk, he had wrestled his necktie free of his collar and unbuttoned his jacket and the top buttons of his shirt, but he still looked uncomfortable in the garments. Truth be told, he hadn't looked comfortable this week in any of his new clothes. He'd always looked as if he wanted to shed the skin of the animal she was trying to change him into. He looked that way now, too.

But he'd asked her to change him, she reminded herself. There was no reason for her to feel this sneaking guilt. She was trying to help him. She *was.* He was the one who had wrecked their afternoon today with his boorish behavior. He even admitted it.

"Why did you do it?" she asked. "We were having such a nice time."

"No, *you* were having a nice time, Ava. *I* was turning into Mary fu—uh… Mary friggin' Poppins."

"But Peyton, if you want to get along in—" somehow, she managed to get the words out "—my world, then you need to know how to—"

"I don't need to know how to *take tea,*" he interrupted her, fairly spitting the last two words. "Admit it, Ava. The only reason you took me to that place was to get even with me for something. For being less than a gentleman—what you consider a gentleman, anyway—at the Art Institute yesterday. Or maybe for something else this week. God knows you're as hard to read now as you were in high school."

Ignoring his suggestion that she'd made him go to the tearoom as a punishment—since, okay, maybe possibly perhaps there was an element of truth in that—and ignoring, too, his charge that she was hard to read since he'd never bothered to see past the superficial—she latched on to his other comment instead. "What *I* consider a gentleman?" she said indignantly. "News flash, Peyton—what I'm teaching you to be is what any woman in her right mind would want a man to be."

He grinned at that. An arrogant grin very like the ones to which he'd treated her in high school. "Oh, yeah? Funny, but a lot of women who knew me before this week liked me just fine the way I was. *A lot* of women, Ava," he reiterated with much emphasis. "Just *fine.*"

She smiled back with what she hoped was the same sort of arrogance. "Note that I said, 'any woman in her *right* mind.' I doubt you've known too many of those, considering the social circle—or whatever it was—you grew up in."

She wanted to slap herself for the comment. Not just because it was so snotty, but because it wasn't true. Right-minded people weren't defined by their social circles. There were plenty of people in Chicago's upper crust who were crass and insufferable, and there were plenty of people living in poverty who were the picture of dignity and decency. But that was the effect Peyton had on her—he made her want to make him feel as small as he made her feel. The same way he had in high school.

He continued to smile, but his eyes went flinty. "Yeah, but these days, I move in the same kind of circle you grew up in. And hell, Ava, at least I *earned* my money. That's more than you can say for yourself. Your daddy gave you everything you ever had. And even Daddy didn't work for what he had. He got it from his old man. Who got it from his old man. Who got it from his old man. Hell, Ava, how long has it been since anyone in your family actually *worked* for all the nice things they own?"

Something in her chest pinched tight at that. Not just because what he said about her father was true—although Jennings Brenner III earned pennies these days working in the prison kitchen, he'd inherited his wealth the same way countless Brenners before him had. But also because Ava still hated the reminder of the way her family used to be, and the way they'd treated people like Peyton. She hated the reminder of the way *she* used to be, and the way *she'd* treated people like Peyton. He was right about her money, too—about the money she'd had back in high school, anyway. It hadn't been hers. She hadn't earned any of it. At least Peyton had had a job after school and paid his own way in the world. In that regard, he'd been richer back then than she. She'd *really* had no right to treat him the way she had when they were kids.

The kettle began to boil, and, grateful for the distraction, she spun around to pour the hot water carefully into her cup. For long moments, she said nothing, just focused on brewing her tea. Peyton's agitation at her silence was almost palpable. He took a few steps into the kitchen, pausing right beside her. Close enough that she could again feel his heat and inhale the savory scent of him. Close enough that she again wanted him to move closer still.

"So that's it?" he asked.

Still fixing her attention on her cup, she replied, "So what's it?"

"You're not going to say anything else?"

"What else am I supposed to say?"

"I don't know. Something about how my money is new money, so it's not worthy of comparison to yours, being as old and moldy as it is, or something like that."

The teenage Ava would have said exactly that. Only she would have delivered the comment in a way that made it sound even worse than Peyton did. Today's Ava wanted no part of it. What today's Ava did want, however…

Well. That was probably best not thought about. Not while Peyton was standing so close, looking and smelling as good as he did.

She sidestepped his question by replying, "Why would I say something like that when you've already said it?"

"Because I didn't mean it."

"Fine. You didn't mean it."

Instead of placating him, her agreement only seemed to irritate him more. "Why aren't you arguing with me?"

"Why do you want me to argue?"

"Stop answering my questions with a question."

"Am I doing that?"

"Dammit, Ava, I—"

She spoke automatically, as she had all week, when she said, "Watch your language."

He hesitated a moment, then said, "No."

That, finally, made her look up. “What?”

He smiled again, but this time it was less arrogant than it was challenging. “I said, ‘No,’” he repeated. “I’m not going to watch my language. I’m sick of watching my language.”

To prove his point, he followed that announcement with a string of profanity that made Ava wince. Then he fairly rocked back on his heels, as if waiting for her to retaliate. No, as if he was looking forward to her retaliation. As if he would relish it.

So, in retaliation, Ava went back to her tea. She dunked the strainer a few more times, removed it from the brew and set it aside. Then she lifted the cup to her lips and blew softly to cool it. When she braved a glimpse at Peyton, she could see that his annoyance had steeped into anger. She replaced her tea on the counter without tasting it. But she continued to gaze into its pale yellow depths when she spoke.

“No more arguing, Peyton. I’m tired of it, and it gets us nowhere.”

He said nothing in response, only stood with his body rigid, glaring at her. Then, gradually, he relented. She could almost feel the fight go out of him, too, as if he were just as tired of the antagonism as she was.

"If I apologize for my behavior this afternoon," he asked, "will you come back to work for me?"

She told herself to say no and assure him that he'd learned enough to manage the rest of the way by himself. But for some reason, she said nothing.

"You said we still have a lot of work to do," he reminded her.

She told herself to admit she'd only said that because she hadn't wanted to end their time together. But for some reason, she said nothing.

"I mean, what if Caroline sets up a date for me and Francesca that involves seafood? I don't know how to eat a lobster that doesn't include slamming it on a picnic table a half dozen times."

She told herself to tell him he should just ask the matchmaker not to send them to Catch Thirty-Five.

"Or what if she makes us go to a wine bar? You and I have barely covered wine, and that's something you rich people always end up talking about at some point."

She told herself to tell him he should just ask the matchmaker not to send them to Avec.

"Or, my God, dancing. I don't know how to do any of that Arthur Murray stuff. I can't even do that 'Gangnam Style' horse thing."

Although that made her smile, Ava told herself to tell him he should just ask the matchmaker not to send them to Neo.

She told herself to tell him all those things. Then she heard herself say, "All right. I'll teach you about seafood, wine and dancing between now and the end of next week."

"And some other stuff, too," he interjected.

She looked up at that and immediately wished she hadn't. Within the passage of a few moments, he'd somehow become even more attractive than he was before. He looked…gentler. More personable. More approachable. Like the sort of man any woman in her right mind would want…

"What other stuff?" she asked, quelling the thought before it fully formed.

He seemed at a loss for a minute, then said, "I'll make a list."

"Okay," she agreed reluctantly. It was only for another week. Surely she could be around him for one more week without losing her heart. *Mind,* she quickly corrected herself. Without losing her mind.

"Do you promise?" he asked, sounding uncertain.

It was an odd request. Why did he want her to promise? It was as if they were back to being adolescents. Why didn't he trust her to follow through? She'd done her part this week to teach him all the things he'd asked her to help him with. It was only when he'd thrown those lessons out the window and turned into a boor that she'd walked away.

"Yes, I promise."

"You promise to help me with everything I need help with?"

"Yes. I promise. But in return, you have to promise you'll stop challenging me every step of the way."

He grinned at that, but there was nothing arrogant or challenging in the gesture this time. In fact, this time, when Peyton smiled, he looked quite charming. “Oh, come on. You love it when I challenge you.”

Oh, sure. About as much as she had loved it in high school.

“Promise me,” she insisted.

He lifted his right hand, palm out, as if taking a pledge. “I promise.”

“This day’s a wash, though,” she told him. “It’s too late to get started on anything new.”

“I’m sorry for the way I behaved at the tearoom,” he said, surprising her again.

“And I’m sorry I made you go to a tearoom,” she conceded.

The remark reminded her she was still wearing her hat and gloves, and she lifted her hands to inspect the latter. She’d seen them in a vintage clothing store when she was still in college and hadn’t been able to resist them. What had possessed her to buy white gloves with more buttons than a lunar module? Oh, right. To match the white dress with more buttons than Cape Canaveral that she’d bought at a different vintage clothing store. She began the task of unfastening each of the pearly little buttons on her left glove.

"No, don't," Peyton said abruptly.

When she looked at him, she saw that his gaze was fixed on her two gloved hands. "Why not?"

Now his gaze flew to her face, and she couldn't help thinking he looked guilty about something. "Uh…it's just…um…I mean…ah…" He swallowed hard. "They just look really nice on you."

His cheeks were tinged with the faintest bit of pink, she noted with astonishment. Was he actually blushing? Was that possible? Surely it was due to the bad lighting in the kitchen. Even so, something in his eyes made heat spark in her belly, spreading quickly outward, warming parts of her that really shouldn't be warming at the moment.

"Thank you," she said, the words coming out a little unevenly.

When she started to unbutton her glove once more, Peyton lifted a hand halfway to hers, looking as if he wanted to object again. She halted, eyeing him in silent question, and he dropped his hand with clear reluctance. *How odd,* she thought. She went back to the task, but couldn't help noticing how he still pinned his gaze to her hands, and how a muscle in his jaw twitched as his cheeks grew ruddier. Where she normally had no trouble removing the garments, for some reason, suddenly, her hands didn't want to cooperate. When the second button took longer to free than the first, and the third took even longer than the second, Peyton started to lift a hand toward hers again, closer this time, as if he wanted to help. And this time, he didn't drop it.

The more his scrutiny intensified, the more awkward Ava felt, slowing her progress even more. At this rate, he and Francesca would be sending their firstborn off to college before she finished with her first glove. Finally, she surrendered, dropping her right hand to her side and extending the left toward him.

"Could you help me out?" she asked, the question coming out softly and uncertainly.

It seemed to take a moment for her question to sink in, as Peyton was still fixed so intently on her gloved hand. Even when he moved his gaze from her hand to her face, he still looked acutely distracted.

"What?" he asked, sounding distracted, too.

"My glove," she said. "The buttons. I'm having trouble getting them undone. Do you mind?"

Color seeped into his cheeks again. "Uh, no. No, of course I don't mind. I'll be glad to do… ah, *un*do…you…I mean *them.* Help you. Undo them. Of course. No problem."

He moved both of his hands to her left one, but he hesitated before making contact. Instinctively, Ava took a step forward, as if doing so would help him close the hairbreadth of space that hovered between their hands. But all that did was diminish to a hairbreadth the space between their bodies, bringing them close enough that she more keenly felt his heat and more fully enjoyed his scent.

Close enough that, this time, Peyton did move closer, completely erasing any space left between them.

As his torso bumped hers, something at Ava's core caught fire. When he closed his hands over her glove, capturing the fourth button between his thumb and forefinger, that fire exploded, sending rockets of heat through her entire body. It was such an exquisitely tender touch, coming so unexpectedly from a man like him, so unlike anything she'd felt before.

Then she remembered that that wasn't true. Years ago, surrounded by girlish accoutrements in the bedroom of a Gold Coast mansion, she'd felt a touch that was just as tender, just as exquisite. That night, when Peyton had curled the fingers of one hand gingerly over her shoulder and skimmed the others along her nape, the gesture had been so tentative, so gentle, it was as if he were touching a girl for the first time. Which was ridiculous, because everyone at Emerson knew he was already hugely experienced, even at seventeen. With a carefulness no teenage boy should have been able to manage, he had begun to soothe her tense muscles.

The soothing, however, had quickly escalated. His touch did more to agitate than to placate, stirring feelings in Ava she'd spent months—years, even—trying to deny. Each stroke of his fingers over her flesh had made her crave more, until her thoughts became a jumble of desire and want and need. Peyton had been no more immune to the touching than she had. Within moments, what had started as an effort to calm erupted into a demand to incite. They'd been on each other like animals, scarcely breaking apart long enough to breathe.

But they'd been kids, she reminded herself, trying to ignore the heat building in her belly—and elsewhere. They'd been at the mercy of uncontrollable adolescent hormones. They were adults now, and could contain themselves. Yes, she was still physically attracted to Peyton. She suspected he was still physically attracted to her. But they were mature enough and experienced enough to recognize the pointlessness of such an attraction when there was nothing else between them to make it last. Sex was only sex without emotion to enrich it. And she was beyond wanting to have sex with someone when there was no future in it for either of them.

Now the caress of his fingers on her hand began to sway her thinking in that regard. Maybe, just this once, sex without a future wouldn't be such a bad thing…

Then Ava realized Peyton wasn't unbuttoning her glove. He was, in fact, rebuttoning it.

"Peyton, what are you doing?" she asked, surprised by how breathless she sounded. Surprised by how breathless she was. "I need you to help me get my gloves *off.*"

He sounded a little breathless himself when he replied, "Oh, I think I like them better on."

"But—"

She wasn't able to complete her objection—she wasn't even able to complete a thought—because he dipped his head to press his mouth against hers. A little gasp of surprise escaped her, and he took advantage of her open mouth to taste her more deeply. With one hand still tangled in her gloved fingers, he pulled her close with the other, opening his hand at the small of her back to hold her in place. Not that Ava necessarily wanted to go anywhere. Not just yet. This was starting to get interesting…

Instinctively, she kissed him back, curving her free hand over his shoulder, tilting her head to facilitate the embrace. When she did, her hat bumped his forehead and tipped to one side. She released his shoulder to pull out the trio of hair-pins keeping it in place, but Peyton captured that hand, too, pulling both away from her body.

"Don't," he said softly.

"But it's in the way."

He shook his head. "No. It's perfect where it is."

They were both breathing hard, their gazes locked, neither seeming to know what to do. The whole thing made no sense. Moments ago, they were arguing, and she was telling him to leave her alone. Yes, they'd ultimately arrived at an uneasy truce, but this went beyond every treaty they'd ever studied in World Civ.

Finally, she asked, "Peyton, what are we doing?"

He said nothing for a moment, only continued to hold her hands at her sides and study her face. Then he said, "Something that's been coming for a long time, I think."

"It can't have been that long. You've only been back in Chicago for two weeks."

"Oh, this started long before I came back to Chicago."

That was true. It had probably started her freshman year at Emerson, the first time she'd laid eyes on the bad boy of the sophomore class. The bad boy of every class. Even before she knew what it was to want someone, she'd wanted Peyton. She just hadn't understood how deeply that kind of wanting could run. Now—

Now she understood all too well. And now she wanted it—wanted him—even more.

Nevertheless, she resisted. "It's not a good idea."

"Why not?"

"Because there's no point in it."

"There was no point in it sixteen years ago, either, but that didn't stop us then."

"That's exactly my point."

He smiled at that. "But we were so good together, Ava."

"That one night we were."

He lifted one shoulder and let it drop. "Most people don't get one night like that their entire lives."

Implicit in his statement was that if they let things continue the way they had started, she and Peyton could have not just one but two nights like that. But was it enough? And wanting him more now, would it be even harder to let him go this time?

She didn't have a chance to form an answer to either question, because Peyton lowered his head and kissed her again. He was more careful this time, tilting to avoid her hat, brushing his lips gently over hers once, twice, three times, four. With every stroke of his mouth, Ava's heart raced more wildly, her temperature shot higher, and her thoughts melted away. The next thing she knew, she was framing Peyton's face in her gloved hands and kissing him back with all the tenderness he was showing her.

But just as before, that deliberation quickly escalated. She pushed her hands through his hair to cup one over his nape and the other along his throat. Then both hands were skimming under his lapels to push his jacket from his shoulders. He shrugged the garment off, then moved his hands to the top of her dress, unfastening the first of its many buttons. She wanted to undo the ones on his shirt, but her gloves hindered her once more. She pulled her mouth away from his to attempt their removal again, only to have him stop her.

"I want them off so I can touch you," she said.

"And I want them on," he told her. He grinned in a way that was downright salacious. "At least the first time. And the little hat, too."

Her pulse quickened at the prospect of a second—and perhaps even a third—time. Just as there had been that night when they were teenagers, even if the third time had been thanks to Peyton's gentle touches, because she'd been too tender to accommodate him again. Touching was good. She liked touching. It had been so long since she'd enjoyed such intimacies with anyone. In a way, she supposed she hadn't truly enjoyed them since that night with Peyton—at least not as much as she had with him. When a woman's first time was with someone like him, it left other guys at a disadvantage.

Then the second part of his statement came

clear, and she couldn't help but smile back. "Just how long have you been thinking about this?"

"All afternoon."

"But I'm having trouble unbuttoning anything with them on," she told him. She hesitated to add that that was mostly because his touch made her tremble all over.

"Oh, that's okay," he assured her. "I can unbutton anything you—or I—want."

He dropped his fingers to the second button on her dress and deftly slipped it free, then moved on to the third. And the fourth. And the fifth. As he went, he moved his body slowly forward, gently urging her toward the kitchen door. Then into the hallway. Then to her bedroom door. Then into her bedroom. He reached her hem just as they arrived at her bed and, with the release of the final button, he spread her dress open. Beneath it, she wore a white lace demicup bra and matching panties. He hooked his thumbs into the waistband of the latter and eased them down over her hips, then gently pushed her down to a sitting position on the bed.

Ava started to scoot backward to make room

for him, too, but he gripped her thighs and halted her.

"Don't get ahead of yourself," he murmured.

He started pulling down her panties again, over her thighs and knees, kneeling to push them along her calves and over her ankles. Instead of rising again, however, he moved between her legs, pushing her thighs apart. When Ava threaded her white-gloved hands through his hair, he gripped one of her wrists to place a kiss at the center of her palm. She closed her eyes, feeling the kiss through the fabric, through her skin, down to her very core. Then she felt his mouth on her naked thigh, and she gasped, her eyes flying open. Instinctively, she tried to close her legs, but he caught one in each hand and opened her wider. Then he moved his mouth higher, and higher, and higher still, until he was tasting her in the most intimate way he could.

Pleasure pooled in her belly as he darted his tongue against her, rippling outward to send ribbons of deliciousness echoing through her. Over and over, he savored her, relished her, aroused her. Little by little, those ribbons began to coil tight. Closer and closer they drew, until she didn't think she would be able to tolerate the chaos surging through her. Then, just when she thought she would shatter, those coils sprang free and she fell back onto the bed, arms spread wide, surrendering as one wave after another engulfed her.

Delirious, panting for breath, she somehow managed to lift her head enough to see Peyton stand. As he moved his hands to the buttons of his shirt, his grin was smug and satisfied. As much as she had enjoyed the last—how long had she been lying here? Moments? Months? An eternity?—she enjoyed watching him undress even more. He did it methodically, intently, his eyes never leaving hers, casting his shirt to the floor and then reaching for the waistband of his trousers.

He might have been a workaholic, but he clearly also took time to work out. His torso was roped with muscle and sinew, and his shoulders and biceps bunched and flexed as he jerked his belt free and lowered his zipper. Beneath, he wore a pair of silk boxers Ava had been in no way instrumental in encouraging him to buy. So either he cared more about undergarments than he did about what he wore over them, or else he wanted to impress someone. She remembered he would be meeting soon with a woman who'd been handpicked for him. And she pushed the thought away. He was with her now. That was all that mattered. For now.

When he stepped out of his boxers, he was full and ready for her. Ava caught her breath at the sight of him, so confident, so commanding, so very, very male. He lay alongside her and draped an arm over her waist, then lowered his head to hers, pushed back the netting on her hat, and kissed her deeply. She curled her fingers around his neck and pulled him closer, vying momentarily for possession of the kiss before giving herself over to him completely. He covered her breast with one hand, kneading gently. Then he followed the lace of her bra until he found the front closure, unsnapping it easily. After that, his bare hand was on her bare flesh, warm and insistent, his skin exquisitely rough.

He moved his mouth from hers, dragging

kisses over her cheek, across her forehead, along her jaw. Then lower still, along her neck and collarbone, between her breasts. Then on her breast, tracing the tip of his tongue along the lower curve before opening wide over the sensitive peak. As he drew her into his mouth, he flattened his tongue against her nipple, tasting her there as intimately as he had everywhere else. Those little coils began to tighten inside her again, eliciting a groan of need.

Peyton seemed to understand, because he levered himself above her and returned his mouth to hers. As he kissed her, he entered her, long and hard and deep. Ava sighed at the feeling of completion that came over her. Never had she felt fuller or more whole. She opened her legs wider to accommodate him and he gave her a moment to adjust. Then he withdrew and bucked his hips forward again. Ava cried out at the second thrust, so perfect was the joining of their bodies. When Peyton braced himself on his forearms, she wrapped her legs around his waist and he propelled himself forward again. She lifted her hips to meet him, and together they set a rhythm that started off leisurely before building to a forceful crescendo.

They came together, both crying out at the fierceness of their release. Peyton rolled onto his back, bringing Ava with him so that she was the one on top, gazing down at him. His breathing was as rapid and ragged as her own, his skin as slick and hot with perspiration. But he smiled as he looked at her, moving a hand to the back of her head to unpin her hat and free her hair until it tumbled around them both.

He was so beautiful. So intoxicating. Such a generous, powerful lover. She'd been thinking she would be able to handle him better as an adult. She'd thought her hormones had calmed down to the point where she would be in control of herself this time. She'd thought she would be immune to the adolescent repercussions of her first time with Peyton.

Wrong. She had been so wrong. He was more potent now than he had ever been, and she was even more susceptible to him. Her control had evaporated the moment he covered her mouth with his. The repercussions this time would be nothing short of cataclysmic. Because where she had responded to Peyton before as a girl who knew nothing of love and little of the workings of her own body, now she responded to him as a woman who understood those things too well. But it wasn't the physical consequences she might worry about in a situation like this—he had slipped on a condom before entering her. It was her heart. A part of her that was considerably more fragile.

And a part that was far more prone to breaking.

Nine

The second time Peyton awoke in Ava's bedroom, he was just as disoriented as he'd been the first time. Only this time it wasn't due to overindulgence in alcohol. This time, it was due to overindulgence in Ava.

Like that first time, he lay facedown, but today he was under the sheet instead of on top of it. And today he was sharing Ava's pillow, because his, he vaguely recalled, had been thrust under her hips during a particularly passionate moment, only to be cast blindly aside when he turned her over. Her face was barely an inch from his, and her eyes were closed in slumber, one of them obscured by a wayward strand of dark auburn. She was lying on her side, the sheet down around her waist, her arm folded over her naked breasts, her hands burrowed under the pillow. She looked tumbled and voluptuous and sexy as hell, and he swelled to life, just looking at her.

Probably shouldn't bother her with that again, though. Yet. A body did need some kind of refueling before it undertook those kinds of gymnastics a second—third? Fourth? They all got so jumbled together—time.

As carefully as he could, he climbed out of bed, halting before going anywhere to make sure he hadn't woken her up. Coffee. He needed coffee. She doubtless would, too, once she was conscious. He located his boxers and trousers and pulled both on, shrugged into his shirt without buttoning it, then made his way to the kitchen. He still couldn't get over the smallness of this place and wondered again where Ava's main residence was. Wondered again, too, why she was so determined that he not find out where it was.

Maybe she would take him home with her, to her real home, now that the two of them had—

He halted the thought right there. There was no reason for him to think today would be any different from yesterday, especially considering the history the two of them shared. The last time he and Ava had spontaneously combusted like that, not a single thing had changed from the day before to the day after. They'd both gone right back to their own worlds and returned to their full-blown antagonism. Nothing had been different. Except that they'd both known just how explosive—and how amazing—things could be between them. Physically, anyway.

Which, now that he thought about it, might have been why they had both been so determined to return to business as usual. It had scared the crap out of him when he was a teenager, the way he and Ava came together that night. Not just because he hadn't understood why it had happened or how it could have been so unbelievably good, but because of how much he'd wanted it to happen again. That had probably scared him most of all. Somehow he'd known he would never have enough of Ava. And talk about forbidden fruit. He'd had to work even harder after that night to make sure he stayed at arm's length.

It hadn't made any sense. He'd still disliked her, even after the two of them made love…ah, he meant had sex. Hadn't he? He'd still thought she was vain, shallow and snotty. Hadn't he? And she'd made clear she still didn't like him, either. Hadn't she? So why had he, every day during the rest of his senior year, fantasized about being with her again? Sometimes he'd even fantasized about being with her in ways that had nothing to do with sex—taking in a midnight showing of *The Rocky Horror Picture Show* at the Patio Theater or sledding in Dan Ryan Woods. Hell, he'd even entertained a brief, lunatic idea about inviting her to the Emerson senior prom.

Sex, he told himself now, just as he'd told himself then. He'd been consumed by thoughts of Ava after that night because he associated her with sex after that night. He hadn't been a virgin then, but he hadn't seen nearly as much action as his reputation at Emerson had made others believe. Adolescent boys in the throes of testosterone overload weren't exactly picky when it came to sex with a willing participant. They didn't have to like the person they hooked up with. They only had to like the physical equipment that person had. Hell, even grown men weren't all that discriminating.

In high school, with Ava, it had just been one of those weird chemical reactions between two people who had nothing in common otherwise. Who would never have anything in common otherwise. Great sex. Bad rapport. There was no reason to think last night had changed that. Yeah, the two of them got along better these days than they had in high school—usually. But that was only because they'd matured and developed skills for dealing with people they didn't want to deal with. Sure, they could burn up the sheets in a sexual arena. But in polite society? Probably still best to stay at arm's length.

Yeah. That had to be why they'd ended up in bed together last night. So it made sense to conclude that today's morning after wouldn't be any different from their morning after sixteen years ago. Except that he and Ava probably wouldn't yell at each other the way they had then, and he was reasonably certain he wouldn't have to climb out the bedroom window to avoid being seen. He was likewise certain that Ava would agree.

A sound behind him made him spin around, and he saw her standing in the doorway looking like a femme fatale from a fabulous '40s film. She was wrapped in a robe made of some flimsy, silky-looking fabric covered with big red flowers, and her hair spilled over her forehead and danced around her shoulders.

"You're still here," she said, sounding surprised.

"Where else would I be?"

She lifted one shoulder and let it drop, a gesture that made the neck of the robe open wider, revealing a deep V of creamy skin. It was with no small effort that Peyton drew his gaze back up to her face.

"I don't know," she said. "When I woke up and you weren't there, I just thought..."

When she didn't finish, he said, "You thought

I climbed out your bedroom window and down the rainspout, and that you'd see me at school on Monday?"

He had meant to make her smile. Instead, her brows knitted downward. "Kind of."

In other words, Ava was thinking last night was a repeat of the one sixteen years ago, too. That, once again, nothing had changed between the two of them. That this morning it was indeed back to business as usual. Otherwise, she wouldn't look as somber as she did. Otherwise, the room would have been filled with warmth and relief instead of tension and anxiety. Otherwise, they would both be happy.

"Coffee?" he asked, to change the subject. Then he remembered he hadn't fixed any yet. "I mean, I was going to make coffee, but I don't know where it is."

"In the cabinet to your right."

He opened it and discovered not just coffee, but an assortment of other groceries, as well. He remembered from his previous visit how well stocked the bathroom was, too. Just how often did Ava use this place, anyway?

Neither of them said a word as he went about the motions of setting up the coffeemaker and switching it on. With each passing moment, the silence grew more awkward.

"So," Peyton said, "what's on the agenda for today? It's Saturday. That should leave things wide open."

For a moment, Ava didn't reply. But she looked as if she were thinking very hard about something. "Actually, I'm thinking maybe it's time to make a dry run," she finally said.

The comment confused him. Wasn't that what they'd done last night? And look how it had turned out. All awkward and uncertain this morning. "What do you mean?" he asked, just to be sure.

She hesitated again before speaking. "I mean maybe it's time we launched you into society to see how things go."

He felt strangely panicked. "But you said we still had a lot of stuff to go over."

"No, you said that."

"Oh, yeah. But that's because there is."

Once again she hesitated. "Maybe. But that's

another reason to go ahead and wade into the waters of society. To see where there might still be trouble spots that need improvement. Who knows? You might feel right at home and won't need any more instruction."

He doubted that. As much as he'd learned in the last couple of weeks, he wasn't sure he would ever feel comfortable in Ava's world, even if they spent the next ten years studying for it. And why did she sound kind of hopeful about him not needing any more instruction? It was almost as though she wanted to get rid of him.

Oh, right. After last night, she probably did. But then, he wanted to get rid of her, too, right? So why was he digging in?

"What did you have in mind?" he asked.

"There's a fund-raiser for La Rabida Children's Hospital at the Palmer House tonight. It will be perfect. Everyone who's anyone will be there. It's invitation only, but I'm sure if news got around that Peyton Moss, almost billionaire, was in town, you could finagle one."

"Why can't I just be your guest?" No sooner did he ask the question than did it occur to him that she might already be taking someone else. His panic multiplied.

Her gaze skittered away from his. "Because I wasn't invited."

His mouth dropped open at that. Ava Brenner hadn't been invited to an event where everyone who was anyone would be making an appearance?

"Why not?" he asked.

She said nothing for a moment, only pulled the sides of her robe closed and cinched the belt tight. She continued to avoid his gaze when she replied. "I, um…I had kind of a falling-out with the woman who organized it. Since then, I tend not to show up on any guest list she's associated with." Before he could ask for more details, she hurried on, "But a word in the right ear will put you on the guest list with no problem."

Wow. It took a brave soul—or someone with a death wish—to exclude the queen bee of Chicago's most ruthless rich-kid high school from a major social event. Whoever organized this thing must have come to Chicago recently and didn't realize what kind of danger she was courting, ignoring Ava.

"Then who's going to put that word into the right ear?" he asked.

"A friend of mine who's attending owes me a favor. I'll have her contact the coordinator this morning. You should get a call by this afternoon."

Of course. No doubt Ava had lots of friends attending this thing who owed her favors that could get done at a moment's notice. Favors to pay her back for not walking all over them at Emerson and grinding them into dust.

"But…"

"But what?" she asked. "Either you're ready or you're not. If we can find that out tonight, all the better."

Right. Because if he was ready, then the two of them could part ways sooner rather than later. And that would be for the best. He knew it. Ava knew it. They didn't belong together now any more than they had sixteen years ago.

"Will you come, too?" he asked.

"I told you. I wasn't invited."

"But—"

"You'll be fine going solo."

"But—"

"You can report back to me tomorrow."

"But—"

"But *what?*"

This time, it was Peyton's turn to hesitate. "Couldn't you come with me as my guest or something?"

He'd thought she would jump at the chance. Wouldn't it be the perfect opportunity to stick it to whoever had kept her off the guest list, showing up anyway? Invited, nonetheless, even if by default? She could swoop in with all that imperiousness that was second nature to her and be the center of everything, the same way she'd been in high school. Peyton even found himself kind of looking forward to seeing the old Ava in action.

But she didn't look or sound anything like the old Ava when she replied, "I don't think it's a good idea."

"Then I'm not going."

She drove her gaze back to his, and for an infinitesimal moment, he did indeed see a hint of the old Ava. The flash of her eyes, the ramrod posture and the haughty set to her mouth. But as quickly as she surfaced, the old Ava disappeared.

"Fine," she said wearily. "I'll go. But only as an observer, Peyton. You'll be on your own when it comes to mingling."

"Mingling?" he repeated distastefully. That sounded about as much fun as *taking tea.*

"And anything else that comes up."

He wanted to argue, but backed down. For now. It was enough that he'd convinced her to come with him to this thing. Okay, to *come,* even if it wasn't technically *with him.* They could work on that part later. What was weird was that Peyton discovered he actually did kind of want to work on that part. He wanted to work on that part very much. Which was totally different from how he'd felt on that morning after sixteen years ago. In a word, *hmm...*

So now that he had the *who,* the *when* and the

what, all he had to do was figure out the *why.* And, most confounding of all, the *how.*

Ava studied her reflection in the mirror of a fitting room at Talk of the Town, feeling the way her clients must. Mostly, she was wondering if she would be able to fool others into thinking this was her dress, not a rental, and that she was rich and glamorous and refined like everyone else at the party, not some poser who was struggling to make payments on the business loan that had bumped her up—barely—to middle class.

That was why most women came to Talk of the Town. To look wealthier and more important than they really were. Sometimes they wanted to impress a potential employer. Sometimes it was for a school reunion where they wanted to show friends and acquaintances—and prom queens and bullies—that they were flourishing. Others simply wanted to move in a level of society they'd never moved in before, even if for one night, to see what it was like.

Fantasies. That was really what they rented at Talk of the Town. And a fantasy was what

Ava was trying to create for herself tonight. Because only in a fantasy would she be welcomed in the society where she had once held dominion. And only in a fantasy would she and Peyton walk comfortably in that world together. Sixteen years ago, that would have been because no one moving in her circle wanted to include him at the party. Today, Peyton was welcome, but she wasn't.

Before Peyton's return to Chicago, Ava hadn't given a fig about moving in that world again. But since his arrival two weeks ago—and making love with him last night—she'd begun to feel differently. Not about wanting to rule society again. But about at least being welcome there. Because that was Peyton's world now. And she wanted to be where he was.

Over the past two weeks, she'd begun to feel differently about him. Or maybe she was just finally being honest with herself about how she'd always felt about him, even in high school. She'd remembered so many things about him that she'd forgotten over the years—things she had consciously ignored back then, but which had crept into her subconscious anyway. Things that, for that one night at her parents' house, had allowed her to let down her guard and feel for him the way she truly felt and respond to him the way she truly wanted to respond.

She'd remembered how his smile hooked up more on one side than the other, making him look roguish and irreverent. She'd remembered how once, in the library, he had been so engrossed in his reading that she'd enjoyed five full minutes of just watching him. She'd remembered how he'd always championed the other scholarship kids at Emerson and acted as their protector when the members of her crowd were so cruel. And she'd remembered seeing him stash his lunch under his shirt one day to carry it out to a starving stray dog behind the gym.

They were all acts that had revealed his true character. Acts that made her realize he was none of the things she and her friends had said about him and everything any normal girl would love in a boy. But Ava had chosen to ignore them. That way she wouldn't have to acknowledge how she really felt about him, for fear that she would be banished from the only world she knew, the only world in which she belonged.

Even with the passage of years and the massive reversal in his fortune, Peyton was still that same guy. He still grinned like a rabble-rouser and could still hone his concentration to the exclusion of everything else. He still rooted for the underdog, and he couldn't pass a busker on the street without tossing half the contents of his wallet into the performer's cup. He hadn't changed a bit. Not really. And neither had the feelings she had buried so deep inside her teenage self.

She expelled a soft sound of both surprise and defeat. Sixteen years ago, she and Peyton couldn't have maintained a relationship because their social circles had prohibited it—his as much as hers. No one in his crowd would have accepted her any more than her crowd would have accepted him. And neither of them had had the skill set or maturity to sustain a liaison in secret. Eventually it would have ended, and it would have ended badly. They would have burned hot and fast for a while, but they would have burned out. And they would have burned each other. And that would have stayed with them forever. Now…

Now it was the same, only reversed. Peyton's success had launched him to a place where he wanted and needed the "right" kind of woman for a wife—the kind of woman who would boost his image and raise his status even more. Someone with cachet, who had entrée into every facet of society. Someone whose pedigree and lineage was spotless. He certainly didn't want a woman whose father was a felon and whose mother had succumbed to mental illness, a woman who could barely pay her own way in the world. He'd fought hard to claw his way to the level of success he had—he'd said so himself. He wasn't going to jeopardize that for someone like her. Not when the only thing she had to offer him was a physical release, no matter how explosive.

Maybe there was emotion, even love, on her part, but on Peyton's? Never. There hadn't been when they were teenagers—he hadn't been able to get out of her bedroom fast enough, and his antagonism toward her for the rest of the school year had been worse than ever—and not now, either. This morning he'd said nothing about last night, had only wondered what today's lesson would be, as if their making love hadn't changed anything. Because it *hadn't* changed anything. At least, not for him.

Nerves tumbled through her midsection as she surveyed herself in the mirror one last time. On the upside, the fund-raiser tonight was one of the biggest ones held in Chicago, so there was an excellent chance she and Peyton wouldn't run into anyone from the Emerson Academy. On the downside, the fund-raiser tonight was one of the biggest ones held in Chicago, so there was an excellent chance she and Peyton would run into everyone from the Emerson Academy.

Maybe if she wore a pair of those gorgeous, gemstone-encrusted Chanel sunglasses…

She immediately pushed the idea away. Not only was it déclassé to wear sunglasses to a society function—unless it involved a racetrack or polo match—she couldn't afford to add any more accessories. As it was, the form-fitting gold Marchesa gown, along with the blue velvet

Escada pumps, clutch and shawl, and the Bulgari sapphire necklace, were going to set her back enough that she would have to exist on macaroni and cheese until July. Still, she thought as she turned to view the plunging back of the dress and the perfect French twist she'd managed for her hair, she looked pretty smashing if she did say so herself.

When she stepped out of the fitting room to find Lucy waiting for her, Ava could tell by her look of approval that she agreed.

"You know, I didn't think the blue shoes and clutch were going to work," the salesclerk said, "but with that necklace, it all comes together beautifully. I guess that's why you're the big boss."

Well, you could take the girl out of society, but you couldn't take society out of the girl. Not that some of her former friends hadn't tried.

The thought made her stomach roil. She really, really, really hoped she didn't see anyone she knew tonight.

"I have to go," she said. "Thank you again for

working so many hours this week. I'll make it up to you."

"You already have," Lucy told her with a grin. "You've made it up to me time and time and a half again."

Ava grinned back. "Don't spend it frivolously."

Not the way Ava had spent so frivolously with this outfit. She wished she'd had the foresight to charge Peyton for expenses.

"Have fun tonight!" Lucy called as Ava made her way to the door. "Don't do anything I wouldn't do!"

Not to worry, Ava assured her friend silently. She'd already done that. By falling in love with a man who would never, ever love her back.

Ten

Peyton paced in front of the Palmer House Hilton, checking his watch for the tenth time and tugging the black tie of his new tuxedo. Ava had been right about the phone call. That morning, she'd called someone named Violet, who said she would call someone named Catherine, and before he'd even left Ava's apartment, his phone had rung with a call from that same Catherine, who had turned out to be someone from Ava's social circle at Emerson—and someone who had treated him even worse than Ava had—gushing about how much she would love it if he would come to their "little soiree." She'd also made him promise to seek her out as soon as he arrived so the two of them could catch up on old times.

As if he wanted to catch up with anyone from Emerson who wasn't Ava. Jeez.

Where the hell was she? She should have been here seven and a half minutes ago. He scanned the line of taxis and luxury cars that snaked halfway down Monroe Street. As if his thoughts made it happen, the door of a yellow cab three cars back opened and Ava climbed out. And not just any Ava. But a breathtaking twenty-four-carat-gold Ava.

Holy crap, she looked— He stopped himself. Not just because he couldn't think of an adjective good enough to do her credit, but because there would be no *holy crap* tonight. Tonight he was supposed to be a gentleman. Tonight, he would be a—he tried not to gag—society buck. Guys like that didn't say *Holy crap.* Guys like that didn't even say *Guys like that.* They said… He racked his brain, trying to remember some of the stuff Ava had taught him to say, since even saying stuff like *stuff* was off-limits when it came to presenting a dignified, articulate image.

Aw, screw it. He could think whatever words he wanted, as long as he didn't say them out loud. And what he thought when he saw Ava gliding toward him, covered in gold and sapphire-blue, was…was…

Huh. Even allowing himself to use his usual vocabulary, he still couldn't think of anything. Except maybe about what she was wearing *under* all the gold and sapphires.

Crap.

Okay, so the past couple of weeks had been the best of times and the worst of times. The best of times because he'd been around Ava, and he now knew how to do things that increased his social value to women like her. But the worst of times because, even with his increased social value, Ava still didn't want him. Not the way he wanted her.

Well, okay, she *wanted* him. At least, last night she had. She had definitely wanted him the way he wanted her last night. She just didn't want him today. Not the way he wanted her. And it was a different kind of wanting he felt today—a way more important kind of wanting—than it had been last night. Which was weird, because last night he'd wanted her in a way that was pretty damned important. What was even worse—in fact, what was the worst part of all—was that she was more firmly entrenched in his head now than ever, and he had no idea how to deal with it. And she wasn't just in his head. She was in other body parts, too. And not just the ones that liked to have sex.

She'd changed since high school. A lot. Yeah, there had been times when she'd tried to shroud herself in the same ice-princess disguise she'd worn in high school, but Peyton had seen past the facade. She was warmer now, more accessible. More fun to be around. Even when the two of them sparred with each other, there was something enjoyable about it.

But then, he'd kind of enjoyed sparring with her in high school, too. Really, now that he thought about it, he realized Ava couldn't have been *that* cold and distant back then. Not all the time. There must have been something about her that attracted him—something only his subconscious had been able to see. Otherwise he wouldn't have been attracted. Since coming back to Chicago, his conscious had started to pick up on it, too. Ava wasn't vain, shallow or snotty. Had she been vain, she wouldn't have thought about anyone but herself, and she never would have helped him out with his self-improvement, even if he was paying her. Why shouldn't he pay her? He was going to pay someone else for their expertise, and hers was even more expert because she'd grown up in the environment he was trying to penetrate. Uh…he meant *enter.* Uh…he meant *join.* Yeah, join.

She wasn't shallow, either, because she knew a lot of stuff about a lot of stuff. Had she been shallow, he could have tallied her interests on one hand. She'd introduced him to things he'd never thought about before, a lot of which wasn't even related to social climbing. And she wasn't snotty, because she'd shared that knowledge with him, knowing he would use it for social climbing, not caring that his new money would mix with old. Not once had she criticized him for being nouveau riche. Only Peyton had done that.

Yep, he definitely knew now what he liked

about Ava. And, at the moment, it was all wrapped in gold and walking right toward him.

"What are you doing out here?" she asked by way of a greeting when she came to a halt before him.

"I'm waiting for you."

"You were supposed to leave my name at the door as your plus-one and go in without me to start mingling. We're not together, remember?"

How could he forget? She'd made clear this morning that last night hadn't changed anything between them. "But I don't know anyone in there. How am I supposed to mingle when I don't know anyone?"

"Peyton, that's the whole point of mingling."

But mingling sucked. It sucked as much as having to tame his profanity. It sucked as much as having to pay ten times what he normally did for a haircut. It sucked as much as not being able to wear ten-year-old blue jeans that were finally broken in the way he liked.

Why did he want to join a class of people who had to do so many things that sucked? Oh, yeah. To increase his social standing. Which would increase his business standing. Which would allow him to take over a company that would increase his monetary standing. That was the most important thing, wasn't it? Making money? Increasing his value? At least, that had been the most important thing before he landed back in Chicago. Somehow, over the past couple of weeks, that had fallen a few slots on his most important stuff in the world list.

Huh. Imagine that.

"Just promise me you won't slip out of view," he told Ava.

"I promise. Now get in there and be the status-seeking, name-dropping, social-climbing parvenu I've come to know and lo— Uh...I've come to know."

Peyton's stomach clenched at the way she first stumbled over the word *love,* then discarded it so easily. Instead, he focused on another word. "Parvenu? What the hell is that? That's not one of those upper-crusty words you taught me. See? I told you we still have a lot to do."

"Just give them my name and get in there," she told him, pointing toward the door. "I'll count to twenty and follow." As he started to move away, she hissed under her breath, "And no swearing!"

Peyton forced himself to move forward, ignoring the flutter of nerves in his belly. He had nothing to be nervous about. He'd been entering fancy, expensive places like this for years and had stopped feeling self-conscious in them a long time ago. Even so, it surprised him when a doorman stepped up to open the door for him, welcoming him to the Palmer House Hilton, punctuating the greeting with a respectful *sir.* Because in spite of all that Peyton had achieved since the last time he was in Chicago, tonight he felt like an eighteen-year-old kid who had never left. A kid from the wrong side of town who was trying to sneak into a place he shouldn't be. A place he wasn't welcome. A place he didn't belong.

The feeling was only amplified once he was inside the hotel. The Palmer House was an unassuming enough building on the outside, but inside it looked like a Byzantine cathedral, complete with ornamental columns, gilt arches and a lavishly painted ceiling. The place was packed with people who were dressed as finely as he, the men in black tie and the women in gowns as richly colored as precious gems. Catherine Bellamy, he remembered. That was the name of his former classmate who had asked him to look for her. Except that now her name was Catherine Ellington, because she married Chandler Ellington, who'd been on the Emerson hockey team with Peyton, and who was the biggest…

He tried to think of a word for Chandler that would be socially acceptable but couldn't come up with a single one. That was how badly the guy had always treated Peyton in high school. Suffice it to say Chandler had been a real expletive deleted in high school. So had Catherine. So they were perfect for each other. Anyway, he was pretty sure he'd recognize them if he saw them.

He followed the well-heeled crowd, figuring they were all destined for the same place, and found himself in the grand ballroom, which was every bit as sumptuous—and intimidating—as the lobby. Chandeliers of roped crystal hung from the ceiling above a room that could have been imported from the Palace of Versailles. A gilt-edged mezzanine surrounded it, with people on both levels clutching flutes of champagne and cut-crystal glasses of cocktails. A waiter passed with a tray carrying both, and Peyton automatically went for one of the latter, something brown he concluded would be whiskey of some kind, a spirit he loved in all its forms.

He took a couple of fortifying sips, but they did nothing to dispel his restlessness. So he scanned the crowd for a flash of gold that was splashed with sapphire. He found it immediately. Found her immediately. Ava had just entered the ballroom and was reaching for a glass of champagne herself. He waited until he caught her eye, then lifted his glass in salute. She smiled furtively and did likewise, subtly enough so that only he would see the gesture.

It was enough. Ava had his back. Taking a deep breath, Peyton turned and ventured into the crowd.

Ava managed to make it through the first hour of the fund-raiser without incident, mostly by tucking herself between a couple of potted topiaries on the mezzanine. That way, she could keep an eye on the crowd below and still snatch the occasional glass of champagne or canapé from a passing server. Even if Peyton moved from one place to another, it was easy to keep an eye on him.

It quickly became evident, however, that he didn't need an eye on him. He was a natural. From the moment he flowed into the sea of people, he looked as if he'd been one of them since birth. She kept waiting for him to make a misstep—to untie his tie or ask a waiter for a longneck beer—but he never did. Even now, he was cradling a drink with all the sophistication of James Bond and smiling at a silver-Givenchy-clad Catherine Bellamy as if she were the most fascinating woman he'd ever had the pleasure to meet.

He'd located her within moments of his arrival—or rather, Catherine had located him—and had yet to escape her. Catherine was clearly taking great delight in escorting him through the crowd, reacquainting him with dozens of their former schoolmates. Peyton had greeted each of them with one of his toe-curling smiles, never once hinting at how appallingly they had all treated him in high school.

If he could manage that, there was no way he needed further instruction in etiquette from Ava. After tonight, she could send him on his merry way without her. Off to be the toast of whatever society he might happen to find himself in. Off to his multimillion-dollar estate that was half a continent away. Off to meet the "right" kind of woman his matchmaker had found for him. Off to live his successful life with his blue-blooded wife and his perfectly pedigreed children. Off to launch his business into the stratosphere and line his pockets with even more money. That was the life he wanted. That was the life he had fought so hard, for so long, to achieve. That was the life he wouldn't sacrifice anything for. He was the master of his own destiny now. And that destiny didn't include—

"Ava Brenner. Oh, my God."

It was amazing, Ava thought, how quickly the brain could process information it hadn't accessed in years. She recognized the voice before she turned around, even though she hadn't heard it since high school. Deedee Hale. Of the Hinsdale Hales. At her side was Chelsea Thomerson, another former classmate. Both looked fabulous, of course, blonde Deedee in her signature red—this one a lush Zac Posen—and brunette Chelsea in a clingy strapless black Lagerfeld.

"What on *earth* are you doing here?" Deedee asked. She never could utter a complete sentence without emphasizing at least one word. "Not that I'm not *incredibly* happy to see you, of course. I'm just so *surprised*."

"What a beautiful dress," Chelsea added. "I don't think I've ever seen a knockoff that looked more genuine."

"Hello, Deedee. Chelsea," Ava said. As politely as she could, she added, "It's not a knockoff. It's from Marchesa's new spring collection." And because she couldn't quite help herself, she also added, even more politely, "You just haven't seen it anywhere else yet. I have the only one in Chicago."

"Ooooh," Chelsea said. "You carry it in that little shop of yours."

"I do," Ava said with almost convincing cheeriness.

"How *is* that little project going, by the way?" Deedee asked. "Are we *still* pulling ourselves up by our little bootstraps, hmm?"

"Actually," Ava said, "tonight, we're pulling ourselves up by our little Escadas."

"Ooooh," Deedee said. "You carry *those* in your little shop, too."

"Yes, indeed."

"Have you *seen* Catherine?" Deedee asked. "I'm guessing she was *very* surprised to find you here."

"I haven't, actually," Ava said. "There are just so many people, and I haven't had a chance to—"

Before she could finish, Deedee and Chelsea were on her like a pack of rabid debutantes. As if they'd choreographed their movements before coming, each positioned herself on one side of Ava and looped an arm through hers.

"But you *must* see Catherine," Deedee said.

"She's been so adamant about speaking to *everyone* on the guest list."

Translation, Ava thought, *Catherine will want to know there's a party crasher among us.*

"And since you so rarely attend these things," Chelsea added, "I'm sure Catherine will especially want to see you."

Translation, Ava thought, *You don't belong here, and when Catherine sees you, she's gonna kick your butt from here to Saks Fifth Avenue.*

Ava opened her mouth to say something that might allow her to escape, but to no avail. The women chatted nonstop as they steered her to the stairs and down to the ballroom, barely stopping for breath. Short of breaking free like a panicked Thoroughbred and galloping for the exit, there was little Ava could do but go along for the ride.

The two women located Catherine—and, by extension, Peyton—in no time, and herded Ava in that direction. Peyton looked up about the same time Catherine did, and Ava wasn't sure which of them looked more surprised. Catherine recovered first, however, straightening to a noble posture, plastering a regal smile on her face and lifting an aristocratic hand to brush back a majestic lock of black hair. Honestly, Ava thought, it was a wonder she hadn't donned a tiara for the event. Her gaze skittered from Chelsea to Deedee then back to Ava.

"Well, my goodness," she said flatly. "Ava Brenner, as I live and breathe. It's been years. Where have you been keeping yourself?"

Ava knew better than to reply, because Catherine always answered her own questions. But unlike Deedee and Chelsea, who at least pretended to be polite—kind of—Catherine, having ascended to the queen bee throne the moment Ava was forced to abdicate, saw no reason to pull punches. Especially when she was dealing with peasants.

Sure enough, Catherine barely paused for breath. "Oh, wait. I know. Visiting your father in the state pen and your mother in the loony bin, and running your little shop for posers. It's amazing you have any time left for barging into events to which you were in no way invited."

Ava had had enough run-ins with her former friends by now that nothing Catherine could say would surprise or rattle her. Or hurt her feelings, for that matter. No, only having Peyton hear what Catherine said could do that. That could hurt quite a lot, actually.

She'd also endured enough encounters with ex-acquaintances to have learned that the best way to deal with them was to look them in the eye and never flinch. Which was good, since doing that meant Ava didn't have to look at Peyton. Imagining his reaction to what Catherine had just revealed was bad enough.

"Actually, Catherine, my father is in a federal correctional institution," she said with all the courtesy she could muster. She lowered her voice to the sort of stage whisper she would have used at parties like this in the past when gossiping about those who weren't quite up to snuff. "Federal institutions are *much* more exclusive than state ones, you know. They don't admit all the posers and wannabes."

Her reply had the hoped-for effect. Catherine was momentarily stunned into silence. Score one for the party crasher. Yay.

Sobering and returning to her normal voice,

Ava added, "And my mother passed away three years ago. But it's so kind of you to ask about her, Catherine. I hope your mother is doing well. She and my mother were always such good friends."

Until Ava's father was revealed to be such a cad. Then Mrs. Bellamy had led the charge to have Ava's mother blacklisted everywhere from the Chicago Kennel Club to Kappa Kappa Gamma.

Catherine looked flummoxed by Ava's graciousness. Anyone else might have, if not apologized, at least backed off. But not a queen bee like Catherine. Once again, she recovered her sovereignty quickly.

"And your father?" she asked. "Will he be coming up for parole any time in the near future?"

"Four years," Ava said with equanimity. "Do give my regards to your father as well, won't you?"

Even though Ava had had little regard for Mr. Bellamy since he'd cornered her at Catherine's sweet sixteen party and invited her to his study for a cocktail and God knew what else.

Catherine narrowed her eyes in irritation that Ava was neither rising to the bait nor whittling down to a nub. Really, being polite and matter-of-fact was the perfect antidote to someone so poisonous. It drove Catherine mad when people she was trying to hammer down remained pleasantly upright instead.

"And it sounds like your little shop is just flourishing," she continued tartly. "Why, Sophie Bensinger and I were talking just the other day about how many crass little interlopers we've been seeing at *our* functions lately. Like tonight, for instance," she added pointedly. "All of them dressed in clothes they couldn't possibly afford, so they had to be rented from your pretentious little shop." She scanned Ava up and down. "I had no idea you were one of your own customers. And it *is* nice of you to clothe the needy, Ava, but honestly, couldn't you do it somewhere else?"

"What, and miss running into all my old friends?" Ava replied without missing a beat.

Now Catherine turned to Peyton. Knowing there was no way to avoid it, Ava did, too. She told herself she was ready for anything when it came to his reaction—confused, angry, smug, even stung. But she wasn't ready for a complete absence of reaction. His expression was utterly blank, as if he were meeting her for the first time and had no idea who she was. She could no more tell what he thought of everything he'd just heard than she could turn back time and start the evening over.

Where Catherine's voice had been acid when she spoke to Ava, it oozed sweetness now. "Peyton, I'm sure you remember Ava Brenner from Emerson." After a telling little chuckle, she added, "I mean, who could forget Ava? She ruled that school with an iron fist. None of us escaped her tyranny. Well, not until her father was arrested for stealing millions from the hedge funds he was supposed to be managing, not to mention the IRS, so that he could pay for his cocaine and his whores. He even gave Ava's mother syphilis, can you imagine? And herpes! Of course they took everything from him to pay his debts, right down to the Tiffany watch Ava's grandmother gave her for her debut, one that had been in the family for generations. After that, Ava had to leave Chicago and go… Well. She went to live with others of her kind. In Milwaukee. You know the kind of people I'm talking about, Peyton, of course."

As if Catherine feared he might not realize she was talking about the very sort of people he'd grown up among—but whom he'd had the good taste and cunningness to rise above—she shivered for effect. And so well had Ava taught him manners, Peyton hesitated only a microsecond before smiling. But his smile never reached his eyes. Then again, neither did Catherine's. Or Chelsea's. Or Deedee's. Wow. Ava really had taught him well.

"Of course I remember Ava," he said as he extended his hand. "It's good to see you again."

Ava tugged her arm free of Chelsea's and placed her hand in his, trying to ignore how even that small touch made her stomach flip-flop. How even that small touch made her remember so many others and made her wish for so many things she knew she would never have.

Before she could even get out a hello, Catherine chimed in again.

"Of course you remember Ava," she echoed Peyton's words. "How could you forget someone who treated you as atrociously as she treated you? And have I told you, Peyton, how very much I admire your many accomplishments since you graduated?"

Still looking at Ava, still holding her hand, still making her stomach flip-flop, he replied, "Yes, you have, Catherine. Several times, in fact."

"Well, you have had so many accomplishments," she gushed. "All of them so admirable. All of us at Emerson are so proud of you. Of course, we all saw your potential when you were a student there. We all knew you would rise above your, ah, meager beginnings and become an enormous success." She looked at Ava. "Well, except for Ava. But then, look how she turned out. A criminal father and an unstable mother, and not a dime to her name." She waved a hand negligently. "But there are so many nicer things to talk about. I'm sure she was on her way out.

If not, we can find someone who will show her the way."

For one taut, immeasurable moment, Ava thought—hoped—Peyton would come to her rescue and tell Catherine she was here as his guest. She even hoped he would ignore every lesson she'd taught him about manners and tell all of them that furthermore, they could all go do something to themselves that no gentleman would ever tell anyone to do. But she really had taught him well. Because all he did was release her hand and take a step backward, then lift his drink to his mouth for an idle sip.

A small breath of disappointment escaped her. Well, what had she expected? Not only was he behaving exactly the way he was supposed to—the way she had taught him to—but it wasn't as though Ava didn't deserve his dismissal. Back in high school, she would have done the same thing to him. She'd said herself that karma was a really mean schoolgirl. After all, it took one to know one.

Very softly, she said, "I can find my own way out, thank you, Catherine." She turned to Peyton. "It really was nice to see you again, Peyton. Congratulations on your many admirable accomplishments."

She was following her own lesson book, turning to make a polite exit, when she thought, *What the hell?* They weren't in high school anymore. She didn't have to stay on her side of the social line the way she had at Emerson. Nor did she have to silently suffer the barbs of bullies as she had at the Prewitt School. She wasn't part of either society anymore. She was her own woman.

And this society had tossed her out on her keister sixteen years ago. She didn't have to rely on them to further her business or her fortune. On the contrary, any success she saw would be because of people who were like her. People who hoped for something better but were doing their best with what they had in the meantime. People who didn't think they were better than everyone else while behaving worse. Normal people. Real people. People who didn't care about social lines or what might happen when they crossed them. care about social lines or crossing them.

She turned back to the group, willing Peyton

to meet her gaze. When he did, she told him, "It isn't true, what Catherine said, Peyton. I knew you were better than all of us at Emerson. You still are. I wouldn't have made love with you in high school if I hadn't known that. And I wouldn't have…I wouldn't have fallen in love with you now if I hadn't known on some level, always, that you were the best there was. That you *are* the best there is."

Catherine had been sipping her champagne when Ava said the part about making love with him, and she must have choked on a gasp she wasn't able to avoid. Because that was when Cristal went spewing all over Chelsea and Deedee, not to mention down the front of Catherine's Givenchy.

"You *slept* with him in high school?" she sputtered. *"Him?"*

That final word dripped with so much contempt and so much revulsion, there was no way to mistake Catherine's meaning. That Ava had sunk to the basest, scummiest level of humanity there was by consorting with someone of Peyton's filthy lower class. That even today, in spite of his *many admirable accomplishments,* he would never be fit for "polite" society like theirs.

Peyton, of course, noticed it, too. As did Catherine, finally. Probably because of the scathing look he shot her.

Immediately, she tried to mask her blunder. "I mean…I'm just so surprised to discover the two of you had a…ah, liaison…in high school. You were both so different from each other."

"It surprised me, too," Ava said, still looking at Peyton. Still unable to tell how he was reacting to what he'd just heard. "That he would lower his standards so much to get involved with a member of our crowd. It's no wonder he didn't want anyone to know about it."

Finally, he reacted. But not with confusion, anger or smugness. Judging by his reaction, he was first startled, then incredulous, then…something that kind of looked like happiness? The flip-flopping in Ava's belly turned into flutters of hopeful little butterflies.

"*I* didn't want anyone to know?" he said. "But you were the one who—"

He halted, looking at the others, who all appeared to be more than a little interested in what he might say next. Gentleman that he was, he closed his mouth and said nothing more about that night in front of them. Nothing else Ava might say was any of their business, either. She'd said what she needed to say for now. What Peyton chose to do with everything he'd learned tonight was up to him—whether he still wanted high society's stamp of approval or whether he wanted anything more to do with her.

If he valued his professional success and the wealth and social standing that came with it more than anything, he would be as courteous as Ava had taught him to be and pretend the last several minutes had never happened. He would watch her leave and continue chatting with his new best friends, even knowing how they truly felt about him. He would collect invitations to more events like this and exchange contact info with like-minded wealthy types. He would field introductions to more members of their tribe, doubtless meeting enough single women that

Caroline the matchmaker would no longer be necessary.

In spite of what Catherine had said, and in spite of the way they all felt about him deep down, he was one of them now—provided he didn't screw up. A full-fledged member of the society he'd so eagerly wanted to join. Even if he was nouveau riche instead of moldy old-moneyed, because of his colossal wealth, his membership in this club would never be revoked—provided he didn't screw up. He had his pick of their women and could plant one at his side whenever he wanted, then produce a passel of beautiful, wealthy children to populate schools like Emerson. Except that Peyton's children would enjoy all the benefits he'd been denied in such a place—provided he didn't screw up. Even if Peyton's past was soiled, his present—and future—would be picture-perfect. He was Peyton Moss, gentleman tycoon. No one would ever openly criticize him or treat him like a guttersnipe again.

Provided he didn't screw up.

"If you'll all excuse me," Ava said to the group, "I'll be going. I've been asked to leave."

She had turned and completed two steps when Peyton's voice stopped her.

"The hell you will," he said. Loudly. "You're my—" the profanity he chose for emphasis here really wasn't fit for print "—guest. You're not going anywhere, dammit."

She turned back around and automatically started to call him on his language, then stopped when she saw him smile. Because it was the kind of smile she'd seen from him only twice before. That night at her parents' house sixteen years ago, and last night, in her apartment. A disarming smile that not only rendered Ava defenseless, but stripped him of his armaments, too. A smile that said he didn't give a damn about anything or anybody, as long as he had one moment with her. Only this time, maybe it would last more than a moment.

He started to wrestle his black tie free of its collar, then stopped a passing waiter and asked him what the hell a guy had to do to get a—again with the profane adjective—bottle of beer at this—profane adjective—party. When the waiter assured him he'd be right back with one, Peyton turned not to Ava, but to Catherine.

"You're full of crap, Catherine." Except he chose a different word than *crap.* "I know no one at Emerson, including you, ever thought I would amount to anything. But, hell, I never thought any of you—" now he looked at Ava "—well, except for one of you—would amount to anything, either. It's not my fault I'm the one who turned out to be right. And furthermore..."

At that point, Peyton told them they could all go do something to themselves that no gentleman would ever tell anyone to do. Ava's heart swelled with love.

Catherine sputtered again, but this time managed not to spit on anyone. However, neither Peyton nor Ava stayed around long enough to hear what she had to say. Catherine was a big nobody, after all. Who cared what she had to say?

As they headed for the exit, they passed the server returning with Peyton's longneck bottle of beer, and in one fluid gesture, he snagged both it and a slender flute of champagne for Ava. But when they reached the hotel lobby, they slowed, neither seeming to know what to do next. Ava's heart was racing, both with exhilaration from having stood up to Catherine's bullying and exuberance at having told Peyton how she felt about him. Until she remembered that he hadn't said anything about his feelings for her. Then her heart raced with something else entirely.

Ava looked at Peyton. Peyton looked at Ava.

Then he smiled that disarming—and disarmed—smile again. "What do you say we blow this joint and find someplace where the people aren't so low-class?"

She released a breath she hadn't been aware of holding. But she still couldn't quite feel relieved. There was still so much she wanted to tell him. So many things she wanted—needed—him to know.

"You were only half-right in there, you know," she said.

He looked puzzled. "What do you mean?"

"What you said about everyone at Emerson. As wrong as Catherine was about you, everything she said about me is true. Every dime my family ever had is gone. My father is a convicted felon and a louse. My mother was a patient in a psychiatric hospital when she died. My car is an eight-year-old compact and my business is struggling. The most stylish clothing I own, I bought at an outlet store. That apartment above the shop? That's been my home for almost eight years, and I'm not going to be able to afford anything nicer anytime soon. I'm not the kind of woman your board of directors wants within fifty feet of you, Peyton."

She knew she was presuming a lot. Peyton hadn't said he wanted her within fifty feet of himself anyway. But he'd just completely sabotaged his entrée into polite society in there. Even if his home base of operation was in San Francisco, word got around fast when notable people behaved badly at high-profile events. He wouldn't have done that if his social standing was more important to him than she was.

He said nothing for a moment, only studied her face as if he were thinking very hard about something. Finally, he lifted his hand to the back of her head and, with one gentle tug, freed her hair from its elegant twist.

"Looks better down," he said. "It makes you look vain, shallow and snotty when you wear it up. And you're not any of those things. You never were."

"Yeah, I was," she said, smiling. "Well, maybe not shallow. I mean, I did fall in love with you."

There. She'd said it twice. If he didn't take advantage this time, then he wasn't ever going to.

He smiled back. "Okay, maybe you were vain and snotty, but so was I. Maybe that was why we…" He hesitated. "Maybe that was what attracted us to each other. We were so much alike."

She smiled at that, but the giddiness she'd been feeling began to wane. He wasn't going to say it. Because he didn't feel it. Maybe he didn't care about his place in society anymore. Maybe he didn't even care about his image. But he didn't seem to care for her anymore, either. Not the way he once had. Not the way she still did for him.

"Yes, well, we're not alike anymore, are we?" she asked. "You're the prince, and I'm the pauper. You deserve a princess, Peyton. Not someone who'll sully your professional image."

He smiled again, shaking his head. "You've taught me so much over the past couple of weeks. But you haven't learned anything, have you, Ava?"

Something in the way he looked at her made her heart hum happily again. But she ignored it, afraid to hope. She'd forgotten what life was like when everything worked the way it was supposed to. She'd begun to think she would never have a life like that again.

"You tell me," she said. "You went to all the top-tier schools. I could only afford community college."

"See, that's just my point. It doesn't matter where you go to school." He gestured toward the ballroom they'd just left. "Look at all those people whose parents spent a fortune to send them to a tony school like Emerson and what losers they all turned out to be."

"We went to Emerson, too."

"Yeah, but we got an education that had nothing to do with classrooms or the library or homework. The only thing I learned at Emerson that was worth anything…the only thing I learned there that helped me achieve my many admirable accomplishments…" Now he grinned with genuine happiness. "I learned a girl like you could love a guy like me, no matter what—no matter who—I was. You taught me that, Ava. Maybe it took me almost two decades to learn it, but…" He shrugged. "You're the reason for my many admirable accomplishments. You're the reason I went after the gold ring. Hell, you are the gold ring. It doesn't matter what anyone thinks of you or me. Not our old classmates. Not my board of directors. Not anyone I have to do business with. Why would I want a princess when I can have the queen?"

Ava grinned back, feeling her own genuine happiness. "Actually, it does matter what someone thinks of me," she said. "It matters what *you* think."

"No, it doesn't. It only matters what I feel."

"It matters what you think and feel."

He lifted a hand to her hair again, threading it through his fingers. "Okay. Then I think I love you. I think I've always loved you. And I know I always will love you."

Now Ava remembered what life was like when everything worked the way it was supposed to. It was euphoric. It was brilliant. It was sublime. And all it took to make it that way was Peyton.

"We have a lot to talk about," he told her.

She nodded. "Yes. We do."

He tilted his head toward the hotel exit. "No time like the present."

Yeah, the present was pretty profane-adjective good, Ava had to admit. But then, really, their past hadn't been too shabby. And their future? Well, now. That was looking better all the time.

Epilogue

Peyton sat at a table only marginally less tiny than the one in the Chicago tearoom Ava had dragged him to three months ago, watching as she curled her fingers around the little flower-bedecked china teapot. No way was he going to touch that thing, even if it might win him points with the Montgomery sisters, who had joined him and Ava in the favorite tearoom of Oxford, Mississippi. It was one thing to be a gentleman. It was another to spill scalding tea on the little white gloves of his newest business partners.

"Peyton," Miss Helen Montgomery said, "you must have found the only woman worth having north of the Mason-Dixon Line. You'd better keep a close eye on her."

Miss Dorothy Montgomery agreed. "Why, with her manners and fashion sense, she could run the entire Mississippi Junior League."

"Now, Miss Dorothy, Miss Helen," Ava said as she set the teapot back down. "You're going to make me blush."

Wouldn't be the first time, Peyton thought, remembering how radiant Ava's face had been that evening in her apartment when he'd asked her to keep her gloves on while they made love. There had been plenty of evenings—and mornings and afternoons—like that one since then. In fact, now that he thought about it, he couldn't wait to get back to their hotel. She was wearing a pair of those white gloves now, along with a pale gray Jackie Kennedy suit and hat that were driving him nuts.

It was their last day in Mississippi. They'd met that afternoon with the Montgomerys and all the requisite corporate and legal types to fine-tune the deal Peyton had been fine-tuning himself for months. Now all that was left was to draw up the contracts and sign them. Montgomery and Sons would stay Montgomery and Sons, with Helen and Dorothy Montgomery as figureheads, and Peyton planned to keep the company intact. In fact, he was going to invest in it whatever was necessary to make the textile company profitable again, and it would become the flagship for his and Ava's new enterprise. Brenner Moss Incorporated would produce garments for women and men that were American made, from the farm-grown natural fibers to the mills that wove them into fabric to the couturiers who designed the fashions to the workers who pieced them together. Eventually, there would even be Brenner Moss retail outlets. And CEO Ava was chomping at the bit to get it all underway.

Miss Helen moved two sugar cubes to her cup and stirred gently. "Now, remember. You all promised to come back in October for homecoming."

Miss Dorothy nodded. "Helen and I are staunch Ole Miss alumnae. It's a very big deal around here."

"Oh, you bet," Peyton promised. "And you'll

both be coming to Chicago for the wedding in September, right?"

"We wouldn't miss it for the world."

For now, Peyton and Ava would be dividing their time between Chicago and San Francisco, but eventually they would merge everything together on the West Coast. She wanted to include Talk of the Town under the Brenner Moss umbrella and open a chain of stores nationwide, but for now had turned the management of the Chicago shop over to her former sales associate, Lucy Mulligan. However, she was grooming Lucy to become her assistant at Brenner Moss once things took off there.

Funny, how Peyton had returned to Chicago for the single-minded purpose of enlarging his business and making money and had ended up enlarging his business and making money…and gaining so much that was way more important—and way more valuable—than any of that.

Who needed high society when everything he'd ever wanted was wherever Ava happened to be?

"By the way," Ava said, darting her attention

from one Montgomery to the other, "thank you both so much for the homemade preserves."

"And the socks," Peyton added.

"Well, we know how cold those northern nights can be," Miss Helen said. "We went to Kentucky once. In the fall. It must have gotten down to fifty degrees!"

"In Chicago, it gets down in the teens during the winter," Peyton said. "But I promise it will be nice when you're there in September."

Miss Dorothy shivered, even though here in Mississippi, in July, it was a soggy ninety-five degrees in the shade. "Honestly, how do you people survive up there?"

Peyton and Ava exchanged glances, his dropping momentarily to her white gloves before reconnecting with hers—only to see her eyes spark. "Oh, we find ways to keep the fires going."

Hell, their fires never went out. He could barely remember what his life had been like before reconnecting with Ava. Just days of endless work and nights of endless networking. And yeah, there would still be plenty of that in the future, but he wouldn't be doing it alone, and it wouldn't be endless. It would only be until he and Ava had time to themselves again.

"You two are the perfect power couple, I must say," Miss Dorothy declared. "Intelligent and hardworking and obviously of very good breeding." With a smile, she added, "Why, you remind me of Helen and myself. You were obviously brought up right."

True enough, Peyton thought. They'd just had to wait until they were adults so they could bring each other up right. Still, in a lot of ways, Ava made him feel like a kid again. But the good parts about being a kid. Not the rest of it. The parts with the stolen glances, the secret smiles, the breathless wanting and the nights when everything came together exactly the way it was meant to be. He'd never be too old for any of that.

"When your new business gets going," Miss Helen said, "you two will be the talk of the town."

"That's our plan, Miss Helen," Ava agreed with a grin. But she was looking at Peyton when she said it. "Well, that and living happily ever after, of course."

Peyton grinned, too. Maybe some people thought living well was the best revenge. But he was more of the opinion that living well was the best reward. And it didn't matter where or how he and Ava lived that made it worthwhile. It only mattered that they were together. Talk of the town? Ha. He was happy just being the apple of Ava's eye.

* * * * *